MW01133695

Iron

Branch

A Civil War Tale of a Woman In-Between

By
Kelby Ouchley

ISBN-13: 978-1463776978
ISBN-10: 1463776977

This book is available in e-book format from Amazon and other fine e-book vendors.

For Amy, forever

Abita

Chapter 1

Some people say I have waited long enough to tell this story, the first seasons of my life with a particular man. Others think the rapture is still too soon. But I will tell it as I know it now, a whole story, not as I knew then before the pieces came home. A place to start is a day in June of 1863. It is important to know that I was an in-between person at that time.

Blackberries were as plentiful as the spring showers that year. Their vines rambled along the rail fences and grew thick on the burned log piles of the new ground. Mr. Carter was fond of blackberry jam. The day before, he and I picked almost three gallons after dinner. I was cooking them down over a fire in the side yard when I saw dust rising in the road to the south. It was a peculiar dust, not big enough for a horse or mule but too big for a person. As it got closer I found myself stirring the berries faster and choking the sycamore paddle harder. Soon I could tell it *was* a man moving slowly in and out of the shadows of the overhanging oak trees. A wren sang her hurry song from a dipper gourd on the porch.

She too was anxious. The man came steady on past the corner of the garden. A leg dragging in the north Louisiana powdered clay made the dust, that and a cane stabbing it with each desperate step.

"Abita," he called my name from the gate, and I recognized this dream person as Lemuel Greenlea. In a heart's beat I was terrified to my soul.

I came to live with the Carters before the moon began singing to my body. I was born in a place the white people called Indian Village thirty miles to the southwest of Iron Branch. My mother was Choctaw and lived there with a small band of her people. The Spanish talkers had invited her grandfather and his brothers to this country many years before. They were warned to beware of treacherous English speakers with their crazy lust to possess all of the land and water. The white men fought battles and made and broke treaties among themselves. When one group of English speakers, Americans, finally claimed victory, they decided there was no room for the Choctaw on the ancestral lands east of the Mississippi River. Most were forced to walk to a new home in a place white men called the Indian Territory. I have heard stories of the death that swept over people on this journey and after they arrived in a land on the edge of rains.

My mother's people had only been in the Ouachita country for one generation then. Few in number, they were mostly ignored by the white authorities. Still they took no chances and shied away from the settlements. My mother told of a boat load of her imprisoned people from the ancestral lands that came up the river going to Arkansas where their long walk would begin. The steamboat stopped at a plantation below Monroe to take on wood that slaves were allowed to sell. In desperation, two Choctaw jumped from the boat and tried to swim the river. The soldier escorts just watched as one boy drowned in the icy water but another escaped. He survived alone in the wilderness for several months before people from mother's village found him as they returned from a salt-making journey. Peter Ittibano was his name. He was from the Okla Falaiah or Tall People Clan, and later he married my mother's oldest sister.

People called my father a "breed." His father was a French Canadian who had floated down the Mississippi to trap beaver and shoot deer for their hides. He stopped in this country called Ouachita, or Big Hunting Ground, by the native people here at the time. He took a woman who became my grandmother as a wife. She spoke an ancient language that Choctaw could not understand, and her few remaining people soon vanished forever.

My father became a hunter also and provided game for the growing number of settlers coming from the East. Twice a year he would stop at my mother's village and leave four deer hides to be tanned and made into his personal clothes. On one such visit he met my mother. She liked him because he always brought four hides and Choctaw know that four is a lucky number. They lay together in her hut during a freezing rain and from his seed came the waves in my hair. His name was Leboeuf and I never saw him.

Mother named me Abita, which means flowing spring or fountain. It was not as some of the Choctaw women believed, that she vainly thought me beautiful. My features are plain. If I have ever possessed beauty, it is only in my skin, unblemished except for four marks. A man once said it was the shade of tupelo gum honey, but his dark eyes saw more of me than was there to be seen. Mother named me Abita because of the ease of my coming. I sprang from her womb like a fountain even before she could prepare the birthing hut. She took this as a sign whose meaning would be revealed some day.

I lived in the village with my mother until I was ten years old. We raised chickens and tended a garden of corn and pumpkins. My days were filled with the cycle of the corn. We did not know of the sweetness of Stowell's yellow corn then; we were satisfied with the old corn of the Choctaw. I helped plant the seed when the white oak leaves were as big as a squirrel's ear. As it ripened I stood watch during the day to protect it from raiding crows and raccoons. In the evenings I tended the staked dogs that took on the night guard. Once, one of the mongrels bit me in the side leaving a white scar and a bad memory. The harvested crop was stored in cribs set atop cedar posts five feet off the ground. For many hours of my childhood I polished the posts with sand rocks to save the fruit of our labors from the white-bellied mice.

Mother was known as a healing woman because of her knowledge of the wild medicine plants. The white doctors would call on her to purchase for their patients the herbs of the forest that could not be found on the pages of thick medicine books. In this way we were able to eat and live happily even though Mother did not have a man.

Living in the village was like having a quilt thrown over my head. I could only perceive the patterns of life that were close and had no understanding of the changes taking place throughout the country. Settlers from the eastern states poured into the hills west of the Ouachita River. They came upstream on steamboats in the winter and spring as the rising waters flushed the overflow swamps in an ancient rhythm. During the droughts of summer and autumn they drove ox carts and six-mule wagons from Mississippi through a vast and mysterious forest to seek Edens free of flood and fever. They brought with them all the many leaves on their trees of life. My mother saw these changes on her visits to Trenton and Monroe to sell cane baskets and ground turtles. In time, she made a decision that could only break her heart.

I do not know how Mother learned of Thomas and Elizabeth Carter. Perhaps they met in town and bartered over a grass sack of sassafras roots. Somehow, in a mother's way she determined they were good people—good enough to have her only child.

For weeks before I left the village my mother tried to prepare me for a new life. She taught me every word of English that she knew and made the other Choctaw do the same. An old man with blue lightning tattooed on his face insisted on teaching me the signs of the four directions should I ever need to find my way home. I know now that I was also told of some things before my time—the matters of women and even the ways of men. It would be years before I could understand their truths. What mother could not tell me was why I must leave. No language held these words.

On the first day of the year that smelled of autumn we walked to Trenton carrying my belongings in a corner-tied blanket. We met the Carters at the steamboat landing late in the afternoon and Mother talked to them for a long while as I watched mirror-scaled minnows dash about in the currents of the riffles. Finally, she turned and looked at me for a moment before quickly walking away. I remember seeing both of her hands opening and closing, opening and closing, as she went over the bank and out of sight.

The river was low and the small sternwheeler lay in the narrow channel across a long mud flat. Mr. Carter picked up my blanket and his wife took my hand and led me down a trail of rough-cut planks to the boat. The screaming whistle startled me, but I was not scared as the backing paddles changed direction and began pushing us upstream. I was in-between.

A rattling fisher bird led the steamboat around the first few bends, stopping to wait for us on her favorite perches. In about two hours the boat pulled in at a crude landing called Loch Lomond on the west shore, and we were the only ones to depart during the brief stop. We walked up the bank and Mr. Carter whistled through his teeth as if he were calling for someone. I had never heard anyone whistle in that manner. No one answered.

A small bayou flowed into the river just above the landing and a wide trail hugged its high bank into the dense forest. We sat under some very tall pecan trees and waited.

Near sunset we heard a trotting horse approaching. Soon a boy came driving up in a buggy pulled by a beautiful Claybank mare. He was only a couple of years older than me and I was amazed at the way he handled the spirited and powerful horse. Mr. Carter said, "Praised be the Lord! He ain't bloated in the melon patch and just an hour late." After the scolding we all squeezed into the buggy. I sat close against the boy breathing in the strong scent of pine smoke on his linsey shirt.

We rode back up the trail along the bayou until we came to a slab-sided cabin. A man, a woman, and three small girls poured out, and I was able to determine from everyone's talk that the boy had spent the day there after carrying the Carters to the landing that morning. The woman gave us some cathead biscuits and we drove on in the darkness.

Before midnight we reached the Carters' home place. The boy let us out and continued on with the restless, silver-maned horse. That is how I came to live with Thomas and Elizabeth Carter on Bayou de l'Outre. That is also how I met their nephew, Minor Barrett, a boy with eyes as dark as mine.

Thomas Carter homesteaded this place in 1840. He left a barren wife in a fresh Georgia grave and fell in with a small wagon train of settlers bound for Natchez. There they loaded possessions and hopes on a steamboat that dodged snags and sandbars up the Red, then the Black, and finally the Ouachita. He chose as his new home a flat piece of land bordering Bayou de l'Outre but free of the yearly backwater floods. The soil was sandy loam, and a windstorm had thrown down many trees, easing the labor to clear a farm field in the wilderness.

The boats continued to bring settlers, and soon all of the "good lands" were claimed. Merchants, preachers, and tavern keepers who only felt safe when God's forest was kept at a distance built the nearby village of Iron Branch along a small stream that ran red with strong minerals.

On a trip to New Orleans to buy a new rifle and glass windowpanes, Mr. Carter met Elizabeth Barrett, a governess looking for a position. She found a husband instead, and he brought her back to a new double-pen log house and an old feather bed. They were not young, but their dreams were ripe and sweet.

Mr. Carter hired two men to clear forty acres behind the house. They sawed the wind-thrown giants from their stumps and rolled the logs into piles to burn. Of the large trees still standing, they girdled the bark of the trunks with axes to starve the leaves. For several years bull-tongue plows weaved among these dead sentinels to prepare furrows for the cotton.

By the time I came to live with the Carters, the fields were clean and the farm was in good working order. A vegetable garden, orchard, and free-ranging livestock fed us abundantly. Corn was grown for meal and feed for the animals while cotton bought the white folks' unnecessary necessities.

I missed my mother and her village, but I liked living with the Carters from the beginning. They were good to me and in time I came to love them. I was taught to be their housekeeper, and Mother's fee for my labor was soon revealed. She had insisted that Mrs. Carter teach me to read and write. Mother had never known a Choctaw that possessed the magic in books.

Elizabeth Carter was a natural teacher. She had sacrificed her youth for the profession, and I was only the last of many students to be fired with her joy for learning. Until I left her home she tutored me four hours a day every day except Sundays. Even as we worked in the kitchen or garden she would drill me in the correct use of the English language. My old thoughts tangled my sentences terribly. She never discouraged my Choctaw words, but as time passed they drifted to distant places in my mind.

Within a year I could write every word in Webster's Blue Backed Spelling Book. Mr. Carter teased me. "Girl, you done kissed the learning stump," he would say. By the time I was fifteen I had won the Annual Iron Branch Scholar's Competition, an honor that had always gone to girls who attended Mount Lebanon Baptist College in Farmerville.

I learned other lessons as well. It still seems strange to me that such an innocent and personal notion as knowledge could stir poison in the heart of another human being.

"Abita," he called again. "It is me, Lemuel. Can I have water? I am injured."

My mind was spinning like a summer dust devil as I ran to the gate.

"Of course, come in," I cried. "But what of Minor?"

His face was close to mine and much older than it was a year earlier. Our eyes locked together and the dread-words came.

"He is shot in the groin in Vicksburg but was alive when last I saw him."

I fell then, sudden and hard, like a steer struck properly with the back of a single-bit ax at slaughter time.

Minor Barrett's father was a brother to Mrs. Carter. He was raised in New Orleans and trained in Nashville as a physician. He married into a wealthy Creole family, and the frequent ailments of their prosperous friends soon made him rich also.

His wife, though, possessed a spirit uncommon in those accustomed to constant luxury. She was an artist and a musician and yearned for adventure. The wilderness stories told by Mrs. Carter during Christmas visits to her brother's only stoked the fire. Before long the Barretts with their young son were residents of Iron Branch.

They built a fine house in the village using pit-sawed lumber of heart pine. The paint on the outside was the color of beech bark, between white and gray. A whole room was filled with books of the world, the medicine books of Dr. Barrett, the art books of his wife, and countless others. Minor said the library filled a wagon and a half when it was brought from the boat. As a girl, I thought this parlor to be the most mysterious and wonderful place in the world.

I never knew Dr. Barrett. The room that later held such magic for me held the casket of its owner within a year of his arrival in this country. He was called out in the night to treat a sick slave woman on a passing steamboat at Alabama Landing. She resisted his help and had to be tied down and cupped. When Dr. Barrett died suddenly the next day other Negroes said she was a hoodoo woman with the power of curses. I still wonder if the devil or Jesus took this man.

Mrs. Barrett buried her husband in a new graveyard facing resurrection east on the point of a sandy ridge that jutted out into the l'Outre Swamp. She marked his grave with a large iron cross and went back to painting misty scenes of forests without people and playing her violoncello. From this time forward, rumors held that Mrs. Barrett purchased unusual amounts of alcohol just to clean the rosin from her strings.

I saw Minor Barrett from time to time after I came to live with the Carters. He would drive his mother out for Saturday dinner if the road was good. Sometimes we would visit them in the village. Unlike most people he would speak to me like I was a whole person. There was a gentleness about him. Then when he was fifteen he went away to school in Philadelphia to study the law books. I did not see him for more than two years.

Chapter 2

The war was slow in coming to Union Parish. My memory of the first sign of trouble was when Mr. Carter began making a special effort to get copies of the weekly Farmerville newspapers. He was particularly curious about the election for president among John Breckenridge, Stephen Douglas, and Abraham Lincoln. When Lincoln won, people said that a war would be fought, but none seemed to worry that it would reach into this place.

I read those newspapers. The war news was confusing. Most of the writers were mad about people in the North telling southern people how to live. Some of the stories were about slavery, and I did not then know much of the wickedness of this. The advertisements of booksellers and patent medicines were more interesting to me.

One Sunday afternoon the police juryman came to talk to Mr. Carter about having his hired men help with the parish roadwork. I churned butter in the breezeway as they sat on the other end of the porch in chairs turned from white oak and covered with deer hide. It was spring because coral honeysuckle was blooming on the side of the corncrib. The man said that the war had started, and there was a call for volunteers to fight the Yankees in Virginia. They talked about the price of cotton going down if it had to be shipped to mills in England and France instead of up north. As the man left, he told Mrs. Carter that he had heard her nephew would be coming home from school for safety reasons. She said she reckoned that was a good idea, and suddenly I did too.

In less than two weeks he rode back into my life on that same Claybank mare. The horse seemed smaller perhaps because Minor was now nearly six feet tall. Most of the boy was gone, and his movements were flowing and pleasing to watch. He still looked into me with eyes as dark as mine. I knew this to be a sign.

Mr. Carter had asked him to help with the lamb shearing on the day that he first touched me. I had been chopping and burning brush all week on the trail to the new springhouse. Smoke from poison vines caused the rash to break out on my arms, neck and face. I made a poultice of jewelweed and sat on an iron rock at the spring to daub at the welts with a piece of raw cotton. Minor came for a drink of water and looked at me with pity. He poured the tonic into his bare hands and skimmed my cheeks with his fingertips. Lanolin from the wool oiled his touch. He rubbed my forehead next, and then standing over me raised the hair from my shoulders to treat the back of my neck, but in a firmer manner. All of this and he left with barely a spoken word between us.

The next day Minor brought me a package of Frangipanni Toilet Powder. The label read, "A Necessity In The Toilet Of Every Lady – It is unrivalled for removing Chaps, Chafes, Blotches, Pimples and other impurities of the skin, rendering it Soft, Clear, Smooth and Beautiful. Price 25 cents." Minor said that he had no intention of allowing a blemish to take up residence on my skin.

From that time on we each looked for chances to be together. The Carters did not forbid me from accompanying him unchaperoned. One night I heard them arguing about me riding horseback astride instead of sidesaddle. Mr. Carter was against it, but his wife expressed her trust in us. She calmed him, and nothing more was said of it.

We usually met on Sunday afternoons. He liked to ride out to the Carters' to visit, and I wished to go into town with them to the Barretts' house instead. The parlor there enchanted me. With the books could be found the latest paintings of Mrs. Barrett and even some by Minor, who had promised his mother to develop this talent. A telescope to pull the moon closer and crystals that turned sunlight into rainbows were placed before a window with one hundred twenty panes, each as large as a writing slate. For hours I would question Minor about these things and the world that he had seen in his travels.

Minor was different from me. His choice was to pace the mare up to the chopping block in the back yard so I could swing up behind him. We would ride for miles along the bayou to discover beautiful places that we called our own. His favorite was the Buffalo Hole, a wide spot of open water on the l'Outre. In most places the bayou was choked all the way across with buttonbush and passable only in pirogues or small skiffs. It was a cabahannosse or duck roost in fall and winter when thousands of squealer ducks poured into the thickets for safety just as the sun set. The Buffalo Hole was named not for the beast but for the giant bottom fish that could be caught on strong silk line and hooks baited with dough balls. The lake was an emerald pool ringed by columns of ageless cypress trees. Wild canaries darted among the ribbons of hanging moss. Here we would walk out over the water on a certain fallen log to sit and talk. The hobbled horse would snort and stomp at deer flies as Minor reached for my feelings. He sought to understand life's passions and looked to me for answers deeper than my learning. I only know that he stirred in me a hunger for him that could not be satisfied on Sunday afternoons. And so we continued in this way throughout the summer and fall.

As months passed there came news of battles to the east. Men from parishes along the Mississippi River hurried to join the South's new army. They were from plantations with slaves, and Lincoln's words threatened them from afar.

The police jury did raise two companies of soldiers in our parish, the Pelican Greys and the Independent Rangers, but just a few boys from Iron Branch left. Most people here were small farmers, and slaves worked only six large plantations. Those that did go early went for adventure and to escape farm labors.

In spite of people's wishes to see the troubles pass them by, we all eventually began to feel the roots of war grow into our lives. The Yankees blockaded the Mississippi River below New Orleans and threatened to capture that great city. Cotton shipments were uncertain, and goods from the North began to get scarce. People in Farmerville held a small "gunboat fair." They gave jewelry, quilts, and silverware to sell at the fair, and the proceeds were sent to New Orleans to help build a gunboat for the Confederate navy. Still people thought the war would not last long.

When I came to, Lemuel was kneeling beside me with a look of panic about him. Mrs. Carter sponged my face with a wet towel.

"Oh Abita, I did not mean to alarm you so. You scared me to death. I thought your heart stopped forever," he said.

On the porch I threw questions at him like a handful of pea gravel. I snatched at his every remembrance of Minor and burned his recollection into my mind.

Finally he said, "That is all I know, Abita. I am sorry."

Mrs. Carter fed him fried ham, squash and eggplant. He would not wait for a ride with Mr. Carter, who was in the back field with the wagon.

"I have walked this broken foot from Mississippi, and it will surely carry me on to Iron

Branch and my mother. I am finished with this war."

At the gate he motioned me to walk with him.

"You know that I must tell her as soon as I get to town," he told me almost as an apology.

I knew those words long before he spoke them. Already I was trying to sort the whirling thoughts in my head into an urgent plan.

The Bible says snakes are evil creatures, but I think King James' preachers were wrong on that account. Snakes are a part of the natural world, and only those things beyond pure nature can bear wickedness. In my life I have only known humans to be capable of black-hearted deeds. The first was Anatilda Tubbs.

Her family was the richest in the community and with seventy slaves farmed eight hundred acres along the bayou on the edge of Iron Branch. The house sat on a ridge overlooking the fields and village. Minor said there was a room for Sawyer and Grace Tubbs and each of their five sons and three daughters with others left over for the many guests. I only saw it from a distance—gray slate roof and wide porches all around, more than I could sweep in a day.

Anatilda was about four years older than me. I met her at the Scholar's Competition when she was eighteen. It was the last year that she could enter, and she had won second place four times but never first. Even then there was talk that she was too old to compete fairly—most girls her age were already married. Others, mostly her friends, said to leave her alone, that she had been a sickly child with hot measles and deserved to win.

The competition was held a few days before Christmas when the boys and girls who went to boarding schools were home for the holidays. All the people in the contest except me had formal schooling. Mrs. Carter talked for hours to convince me to enter. She insisted that I could do well. As much as I loved her though, I knew I was in-between and not as smart as the town people.

Dew formed on the inside of the windows of the schoolhouse that night and ran down the ledges in trickles. It was warm and muggy for December. A low ground fog hollowed the street voices and split candlelight into circles of rainbows.

Mr. Laran who owned the *Farmerville Democrat* was in charge. In front of the crowded room he clutched to his breast a leather case containing the questions. A company in Louisville that printed books sponsored the contest across the country every year and made the questions. Mr. Laran said that he had to swear in writing to be honest in running the contest. He said more times than was necessary how great an honor it was for the book company to pick him. I always figured he had the easiest part.

Judge Hezekia Thacker, the district judge with a good name for a judge, sat on the front row with some other important men from Farmerville. The Scholar's Competition was an important social event in this part of the parish, an occasion to drum up business, and for the judge decorated with an explosion of gray whiskers a place to harvest votes for future elections. I chose the judge's unusual face upon which to focus my gaze in order to blur the daunting crowd.

There were two groups of competitors—those under twelve years old, and children twelve and older. Miss McMurray, the Iron Branch schoolteacher, chose her ten best students for the younger group. Few older children went to school and only eight including me showed up to enter that night.

Miss McMurray had a linen bag that held fifty numbered walnuts. Mr. Laran had two question booklets that each had fifty numbered questions. One of the booklets had easier questions for the smaller children. Each person drew a nut and had to answer the question with the matching number. It was like a spelling bee except it took two wrong answers to be eliminated. The younger children went first.

Mothers and fathers and brothers and sisters cheered and groaned as one by one the contestants hung their heads and walked from the arena. Mr. Laran sat on a tall stool and passed judgment like a scarecrow king until only one red-haired boy was left. Then it was our turn.

The schoolhouse was so full that one person had to leave before another could come in. It seemed to me that most of them were Anatilda's kinfolks the way they hollered for her and one of her brothers. He was younger than her and looked as scared as me. One other boy and four more girls crowded into a line with us across the front of the room like a row of baby jaybirds on a sweetgum limb. Mr. and Mrs. Carter sat in the back of the room. I wanted to run into their arms and out of this people place, but Mr. Laran coughed, rapped his gold-headed cane on the floor, and tried to begin the contest with educated words.

Four people went out at the end of the second round, and of the four remaining, all girls, only Anatilda had not missed a question. My first drawing required me to spell the word "pernicious," which was easy for me. Hope quickly dimmed though when next I was asked to name the first postmaster general of America. I could only mumble that I did not know.

At the end of the sixth round only Anatilda and I remained standing, and she still had a perfect score. Miss McMurray motioned for us to move closer together at the front of the room, and there for the first time I sensed the disgust that Anatilda had for me. She scowled and pointed her chin at the rafters as if to signal that standing too close to me would somehow soil her and her New Orleans dress.

Mr. Laran turned to Anatilda and continued, "According to Greek legend, who was the goddess of war and wisdom?"

In a quick voice she answered, "Helen, of course."

Mr. Laran raised his eyebrows and looked surprised.

"I'm afraid that is incorrect Miss Tubbs."

Some of the air went out of her crop then but only for a moment as her friends cheered to encourage her.

Suddenly Mr. Laran seemed anxious to finish this matter. He hopped down from the stool in the corner and stood behind the big teacher desk.

"What body of water divides the sands of Egypt and those of Arabia?" he asked loudly.

Mrs. Carter's book of colored map plates appeared clearly in my mind. I shut my eyes and turned the pages until the one with the words "Holy Land" lay open in my lap. When I gave Red Sea as the answer I could have just as easily named a dozen towns on its salty shores.

People in the room did not cheer. Their murmurs seemed to say that something was happening here that they could not understand— perhaps that was not supposed to happen.

Anatilda reached into the bag again and Mr. Laran read, "What famous Indian fighter later became the seventh president of our country?"

She adjusted her Grenadine shawl, turned to glare at me, and spit out the reply to the only question in the contest that most of the people in the room could answer.

"General Andrew Jackson," and then looking out over the room she said, "He put those savage heathens in their proper places."

Judge Thacker slapped his own knee and slapped it again for good measure. His eyes narrowed to show that there was no mirth in this spontaneous gesture. A raw nerve had been poked.

Today I cannot remember the next question. Mrs. Carter said that I gave the answer "William Shakespeare" and that it was correct. I know that for long minutes I could only hear the rushing sound of blood deep in my ears. And in my young throat for a brief moment I tasted the hatred in which Anatilda swam.

She calmly handed Mr. Laran another walnut.

"The Bastille played a critical role in the late French Revolution. What was its original intended function?"

She cleared her throat to announce the answer that would surely and finally prove her station in this village—but it would not come. For long seconds it would not come and a breeze seemed to blow the spreading fear from the faces of her friends across the room and over her. It showed in her eyes and drifted to Mr. Laran, who almost begged for the answer.

"Miss Tubbs?"

Anatilda did not know the answer, and in her way she tried to force one.

"It was the king's castle."

Mr. Laran removed his too-big hat and confessed, "It served as a prison, I'm afraid," and quickly added, "but this competition is not decided until the other contestant successfully completes the round."

I chose a walnut from the bottom of the sack. It was painted with the number four. Mrs. Carter stood up at the back of the room and clasped her hands to her lips. I looked into Judge Thacker's eyes, but in my side vision I clearly saw Mr. Laran turn to the back of the booklet, far past where question number four should be. The judge caught his own hand in mid-air just in time to prevent another knee slapping.

"This is a two-part question. Who is the author of *Twice Told Tales* and who wrote the novel *The House of Seven Gables*?" he demanded.

I felt free, free to leave this place at last. I had never read the books but saw them often. With *The Scarlet Letter* and bound in red leather they sat to the left of Dr. Barrett's sun window on the third shelf from the floor.

"Nathaniel Hawthorne wrote them both, sir."

Before that night I was but a grass sparrow to Anatilda. I lived in the corners of her vision flushing in a blur from the roadside as she traveled through life. It was unthinkable to her that anyone lacking bright feathers could have a song.

When Mr. Laran handed me the prize pewter cup in disgust, I became to Anatilda the snake of the Bible. From that time on I was vermin and was treated as such.

Chapter 3

In late April of 1862, New Orleans fell to the Yankees, and though the nearest enemy soldiers were many miles away, the people of Bayou de l'Outre were finally singed with the heat of war. The big trade boats suddenly stopped coming. The Tubbs and their friends were deprived of fresh oysters for their parties, and we watched the coffee and flour barrels empty away. Plantation owners and small farmers alike wondered aloud about the fate of the cotton crop without a New Orleans market. Those who were smart began to turn inward toward the land for survival. Many could have used lessons from my mother.

Except for Mrs. Barrett, the religious people of this place were not Catholic. They sought God and His miracles most eagerly in late summer when the crops were laid by. Under brush arbors traveling preachers would try to set afire the faithful and wrestle with sinners for a week at a time. Because of the war some people decided that they could not wait until August for God. The brush arbor meetings were moved up to May, and two Arkansas preachers were called.

A natural meadow on the south edge of Iron Branch served as the meeting grounds. From the main road a trail barely wide enough for a wagon forked away at the blacksmith shop and led down to a flat open area surrounded by white oaks and beech trees. An open frame of cedar posts, taller than I could reach, covered most of the small field. Saplings connected the tops of the posts, and green brush was piled on above to make the shade. Split log benches could sit a hundred people at a time. A row of hitching posts lined one edge of the meadow across from long rough tables that often bowed under the weight of the faithful's food.

The meetings began on a Monday night. Since most people were working their crops the services started at six o'clock instead of noon. The Carters and I took the wagon as soon as the milking and evening chores were done. We got to the grounds early and visited with folks until near sunset. Minor and I had planned to meet, and when he came we sat on a bench near the back. Just before dark four pine knots were lit and placed on poles at the front of the brush arbor. Each had a boy to tend it, to keep it going, and to watch for stray embers. The preachers were late and did not make their entrance until full dark. When they did it was a sight worth seeing.

They were as different as a water roach and a horsefly. Reverend Bloomer was a giant and weighed more than three hundred pounds. He was bald-headed and had a black bushy beard down to his belt. The Bible that he carried was the biggest book I had ever seen. He toted it in front of his belly like a treasure chest.

Preacher Snearly was tall too, but he was skinny as a sapling. His thin face was shaved except for a small pointed goatee, and his long hair was straight and white as snow. Bloomer's skin was dark but Preacher Snearly's reminded me of flour paste, and you could see blue blood veins on the side of his head. His Bible was no bigger than a deck of cards. They both wore gold rings, tall black hats, and black suits that rarely visited a wash pot.

In his deep voice Reverend Bloomer started the meetings by shouting, "Brothers and sisters, rise up off these benches and pray with me for eternal peace in this world as we walk toward eternal salvation in the next."

He did not stop for an hour. When he did we sang hymns for a while. I always liked to sing the hymns—except the blood songs—I never sang them.

The torches were crackling and popping when Preacher Snearly started his sermon. His voice was the strangest I have ever heard. It was a loud whispering hiss that carried to the edges of the meadow. He began by talking about the marks of an evil man. He spoke of greed, jealousy, and intolerance. Although he did not say it directly, it was easy to see that Yankees were the targets of his poison. Reverend Bloomer backed him with three-syllabled "a-ME-ins" at every chance.

The preachers traded sermons two more times and we did not get home until after midnight. The best part for me was being with Minor.

It rained hard the next day, and we did not go for two nights because the roads were still bad from the wet season. By Thursday both preachers were leading a charge against anything to do with the northern states. The air was full of amens as first one and then the other bellowed or hissed eternal damnation on all "bluebellies" and their offspring for a hundred generations. Anatilda was there with most of her family on the front row. For a while Preacher Snearly seemed to have her in a trance.

Friday was a full moon night, and Minor did not go to the meetings. He went stovepiping on the bayou with Lemuel Greenlea and would not take me along. He said he had promised to take Lemuel on this moon for weeks, and that he had rather take me in June when we could go alone. "Besides," he said, "the fishing will be better then."

I did not want to go to the meetings either without Minor, but Mrs. Carter asked me in a nice way and I felt obliged. I do not remember much about the sermons that night. The ranting droned along with the rise and fall of the locust calls. There were many blood hymns.

When Reverend Bloomer got up for his last preachin' of the evening, I slipped out the back of the arbor to be away from the crowd for a while. I was thinking of Minor wading among the cypress trees in the clear shallow water of the bayou. I knew Lemuel was holding the pine torch high as they searched the sandy bottom for beds of nesting sunfish. I had been with Minor once before when he slipped the piece of stove pipe down over the nests and reached in to pull out blue and orange bull bream glistening in the torchlight. I knew the grass sack would be heavy well before dawn.

The scent of sweetbay flowers drifted in the shadows as I walked away from the people and along a small creek behind the eatin' tables. The full moon was high, making it easy to see if you did not look back at the torches. I had stopped by a beech log to sip a handful of water when strange sounds began to come into my ears. At first I thought it was a mother coon and her babies talking as they hunted along the creek. I began to move toward the noise in a quiet way that an old man had taught me as a small child in Mother's village. Soon I could tell that the sounds came from the backside of an old falling-down smokehouse, and it was not raccoons. Silently I slipped up to the corner of the smokehouse and peeped around at a sight I will never forget. Anatilda was sitting on a flour barrel and leaning back against the smokehouse with both knees as high as her chin. Preacher Snearly was standing close against her with his bare legs shining blue in the moonlight. The noises they were making could have been from Heaven or Hell.

The sight addled me for a moment, and I could not move. When finally I jerked back I thought Anatilda saw me, but I did not know for sure for another month.

After the brush arbor meetings the war continued to steal closer to us on furtive wings. Every day brought confusing new rumors. In the morning we would hear of a great victory for the South, and before dark another would declare a bitter defeat for us on the same battlefield. A Confederate colonel from the "Bell Battery" came through Iron Branch pleading for plantation bells that could be melted down and forged into cannon. The Tubbs had the only brass bell, and they gave it up with great ceremony. Then the Yankees captured Memphis and Baton Rouge. Vicksburg was the next target, and people fleeing their homes along the great river began passing on the road in front of our house. This trickle of men, women, children, white and black, became a flood in times to come. For now though, the new conscription laws worried me the most.

I did not want Minor to go to the army to fight a war that I could not understand. I did not feel threatened here by Yankees, who the fire-eaters described as demons from the underworld. I could not see an enemy worthy of Minor's bravery, and I dared not think of losing him. As it turned out the greatest peril for us spent her days tatting and playing hull-gull on a wide breezy porch.

After a wonderful Sunday afternoon of visiting with Minor and his mother in the magical parlor, he and I left in the buggy for the Carters' farm. Just on the edge of the village a surrey suddenly dashed in front of us from a side trail. It was Anatilda and her driver Mink. The frightened Claybank mare reared wild-eyed and nearly fell over sideways in the ditch. When she came down she struck out at the other horse with a forefoot. Mink, in one smooth motion with his whip, lashed open the skin on the side of the mare's head. Before he could recover, Minor was on him and they crashed into the red clay road. In a moment Minor had two wraps of the whip around Mink's neck and tightened it until his eyes bulged. Minor dragged Mink upright to a small hickory and tied him standing to the tree by making more wraps around the trunk. All the while I managed to separate the horses, and Anatilda was screaming.

Minor was angrier than ever I had seen him.

He roared at her, "What is the meaning of this?"

She begged him, "Don't kill him! Please don't kill him!"

The talk was that Mink was a half-brother to the Tubbs children. As Minor loosened the whip I could see that it might be true. His skin was the color of café au lait, but his eyes were green and his short hair the dingy yellow-brown of oak flowers, just like Anatilda's. He slid down the trunk and sat there cowed.

Anatilda gathered herself then. The self-righteousness flowed back into her being, and she bloomed like a morning-glory once more.

"Minor Barrett, I have a prospect for you." Her pointed chin no longer quivered. Confidence returned to the voice that whined more often than not.

"What do you want?" he demanded through clinched teeth.

"It seems that your domestic friend here is soon to be encumbered with serious problems."

"What are you talking about?"

"Our good friend Preacher Snearly is back in these parts and is staying at our house until his next calling. He has confided in me events that I find most shocking. He is deeply disturbed and in order to cleanse his soul stands ready to declare the whole matter in a public forum from the pulpit."

"What has this to do with Abita?"

"Preacher Snearly is primed to tell the world that he was seduced by Miss Half-breed Scholar here at the recent meetings."

She turned to me for the first time as she said this. Minor looked at me too. He was as stunned as I. Then his rage began to rise again.

"You are lying!" he said.

She stepped from the buggy and walked to him.

"Am I now? Whether you believe me or not is hardly relevant at this point. Preacher Snearly is a very pious and highly respected man in this country. His word is the gospel truth you know."

She was in control now. Minor's strength was no match for her poison.

"There is however a solution to this predicament—a way to eliminate further embarrassment to all the concerned parties."

"What do you want?" asked Minor.

"Preacher Snearly always seems anxious to heed my advice, and I'm quite certain that I can convince him to lay the matter aside. I do ask one favor in return though."

She reached and took Minor's hand.

"Marry me, Minor Barrett."

In my mind I was not in this drama. I was standing to the side watching it unfold, unable to believe the words coming from her mouth. I could not have spoken had my life depended on it.

Minor jerked away from her as she continued.

"You can never have her Minor. If Preacher Snearly talks she will be disgraced forever. People will drive her away, perhaps back to the Indians to live in a grass hut for the rest of her life. If you really care for her you will marry me and save her reputation. She still will be able to make a life for herself in a white world. Otherwise she is doomed."

Anatilda motioned for Mink to get in the buggy and then walked over to me. An ivory cameo on a black ribbon hung from her neck and she smelled unnaturally of roses.

"Do you think you love him? Love is an emotion restricted to civilized human beings you know. I suppose that you might be capable of some primitive, rudimentary feelings only slightly above the urge to procreate. If so, would you have Minor known as one who associated with the likes of a Babylon whore? From this point on your capacity to love is on trial."

She got into her buggy.

"Preacher Snearly is a distressed man, Minor. I'm not sure how long I will be able to console him. Let me know of your decision soon."

They rode off leaving Minor and me to sort through the hailstones of this sudden summer storm. In a while we drove on toward the Carters'.

Minor said, "She is mad! She has been bitten by one of her father's own rabid, blue-blooded hounds! How could she dream up such a story?"

I told him then what I knew of Anatilda and Preacher Snearly. It became clear that Anatilda controlled the preacher, and with the threat of accusing him of seducing her she could demand anything within his power and get it. Involving me in a lie would only be a small transgression for Preacher Snearly at this point.

Minor became solemn and did not talk again until we neared the Carters'. "It is beginning to make sense," he said. "Jealousy is only one of many lures in her witch's kit, and my fondness for you is the purest of baits." Minor told me that Anatilda had been stalking him since the brush arbor meetings. He said that on the second night when I stayed home because of the bad roads, she insisted on sitting close by him, crowding him hard against the cedar post when the torches burned low. He rebuffed her when she touched him in a manner that a lady would never touch an unfamiliar man. Minor said that she tried to entice him into the shadows with promises that he could not speak of without suffering extreme embarrassment. A sudden, exciting curiosity tempted me to press him for details, but it passed when Minor said that only the day before Anatilda confronted him in the Iron Branch mercantile shop. She publicly implored him to carry out for her the last bolt of cloth in the store, even as Mink stood with the surrey. Minor obliged her and in recounting the scene suddenly lost his shyness. "Pennyroyal tea!" he exclaimed. "There in the street as God is my witness she whispered to me that I had nothing to fear from a vigorous encounter, as she would promptly dose herself afterwards with pennyroyal tea. 'Oh, why tempt ye me, ye hypocrite?'"

At the gate he squeezed my hand and told me not to worry. He said that he would think this out and drove away.

Lemuel passed on the road during the week and brought me a note from Minor saying that he would call on Sunday afternoon. Mrs. Carter and I were busy in the garden at this time. It seems strange now, but I was not worried as I went about my chores. I was not afraid of Anatilda's lies as they pertained to me and thought she could certainly not devise a test of our love. I did not see the problem as it really was.

Minor came on the mare on Sunday. I mounted behind him and we rode to the springhouse where I had left a small, early melon to chill overnight. The saddlebags were bulging and I had to hold the melon in my hands as we rode. When I asked Minor what was in the saddlebags, he spoke in riddles. He said that it was me, Abita, strapped inside the fine English leather cases that had once belonged to his father.

We rode toward our place on Bayou de l'Outre. It was a good five miles from the house through a rolling hill forest yet to feel the sharp blade of an ax. A person could see a long distance under the giant oaks, hickories, and short-needled pines. The settlers burned the underbrush regularly, as had the Indians before them, to make travel and finding game easier. Now, in the summer, the wild pea vines with pink and blue flowers grew on the forest floor and called for the large black bees. Toadstools were plentiful after the recent showers, and only a few had not been bitten by squirrels and ground turtles. The ears of the mare showed us a newborn fawn lying tight to the earth against a log and as still as death. The only noise was the footfall of the mare in dry leaves and the warning calls of jays high in the trees.

The final hill had lost a struggle with the bayou as timeless floods had carved a bluff face in the iron rock and clay. Shade from beech trees on a narrow shelf against the bayou cooled the small cliff enough to grow waist-high ferns. A spring ran steady from beneath the roots of a sweetbay. Long undercut by thunderstorm currents, a cypress had fallen in mid-life and lay stretched from the bank nearly across the bayou. This was the place, our place, on Bayou de l'Outre, to which we came that day.

Minor pulled the bridle and saddle from the horse and cross-lined her to graze in the lush water grass as I spread a quilt near the spring. We took off our shoes and walked the cypress log to its first broad fork. Facing each other and sitting straddle of the log we let the coolness in its journey flow around our feet and legs. Minor cut the melon and fed me pieces from the point of his knife. I traced the moles on his arms and neck and across his breast beneath his open shirt. He considered them blemishes and proclaimed me flawless. I told him of the childhood scar from the dog bite, which had settled on my side at the top of my hip as the bones had broadened. He put two fingers there and held them until after a while he suddenly grew restless.

"I must liberate another beauty from the confines of the saddlebags. Come sit on the quilt."

He took my hand and led me to the bank. I watched as he removed a small canvas, paints, and brushes from the pouches. He trimmed a mulberry sapling to hold the canvas and prepared the oils.

"Do not be afraid."

He positioned me on the quilt looking away over the bayou. Gently and from behind he pulled my cotton blouse up to bare the small of my back. He twisted the shirttail and gave me the knot to hold in front. My hair was yet to suffer the consequences of grief and fell below my waist. This too he arranged to his satisfaction.

Minor demanded of the canvas, "Yet as eons have passed to create this scene primeval, it is only as a moment before such splendor will grace this bayou again. Come forth."

He painted for a long while, and my thoughts were of the present. I could not bear to think beyond this hour of happiness though I did wonder if a heart could suffer to be so full forever. When he finished he held me close and looked through my eyes until I was afraid he would see too much. We danced to music beyond hearing until the shadows grew long.

Minor held the wet canvas carefully on the mare's withers as we rode home. At the picket gate he helped me down and said these words, "My dear, there is but one way for now. I must marry Anatilda."

He kissed me on the mouth and pressed into my hand a small degaurrotype of himself. Carrying my image he rode off into the twilight. Just before he went out of sight the horse snorted twice at the blur of a rabbit darting across the road.

I did not sleep that night. The next day I sat in the swept dirt along the bois d'arc hedge in the side yard from sunrise until the quarter moon rose from the chimney. Before me the ground was covered with the button-size pits of doodlebug traps. As a happy person I would spit on a broom straw and stick it in the hole hoping to catch the insect within while singing a child's rhyme. But on this day I dropped black sugar ants into the pits and watched them struggle until the pincer-jawed creatures snapped them to pieces.

Chapter 4

I learned the particulars of the wedding at a later time.

Minor told Anatilda he would marry her in a month and then immediately go to join the army. He spoke to her father who seemed happy to finally discover a husband for his seasoning daughter. They agreed that the very short courtship was proper only because of the urgency of the war. The wedding was set for a Saturday in July at the Concord Church on the Marion Road.

My behavior caused the Carters to believe that Minor and I had had an argument. This lasted until Minor's mother rode out alone and told them the news. She was distraught and thought the devil was involved in the situation. Mrs. Carter in her way twisted her dish rag and said little to her sister-in-law. Mr. Carter cussed Minor hard and stomped away from the table. He kicked a half-grown cat on the back steps and went to look for grass worms in the cotton. Minor's mother gave me a small book of poetry and said she was sorry before leaving. I buried the broke-backed cat and the book under a China-ball tree later that evening.

The Carters did not go to the wedding of their nephew even though Anatilda sent them and me an invitation on a card stamped with colored flowers. Lemuel was Minor's best man, and the maid-of-honor was Anatilda's cousin from Alabama. All the wealthy people came. Mr. Laran came from Farmerville to write about it in his newspaper. They said the bride was very beautiful in a long silk dress. Mrs. Tubbs and the sewing slaves made it from drapes and old lace because new, fine cloth was impossible to get. I asked Lemuel if it was white, and he said it was.

On the morning of the wedding I went to the springhouse soon after the early chores. I slid the top aside seeking my reflection, but the sun was not high enough to touch the surface of the ever-cool water. There was only a dark shadow in the wooden box. I ran back to the house and returned with Mrs. Carter's looking glass. I brought its tortoise shell frame close to my face to see what Minor could see when he held me close. I knew what he would see when he held Anatilda. Holding the mirror in an awkward manner I also tried to see the nape of my neck and the furrow in the small of my back that Minor had painted. Until this time I had never considered beauty as a thing to be concerned about. It seemed only natural to be satisfied with the body loaned to me by God. Now, the reasons for Minor to marry Anatilda that I had coaxed from my mind became twisted again.

The wedding party returned to the plantation for a mid-day feast. A beef and hogs were roasted. Platters of garden vegetables were served. The last of the cane molasses was baked into cakes and other sweets. They ate on sawhorse tables on the wide porches while two Negro children shooed flies with split-cane fans. After the meal the ladies walked arm in arm down the shady lane in front of the big house. The men leaned against the walls in straight-back chairs with deer-hide seats and smoked Mr. Tubbs' long cigars. Mrs. Tubbs insisted that the united couple dance on the lawn. A sable fiddler scratched out a waltz as they performed to everyone's satisfaction. "Did he look into her eyes then?" I asked of Lemuel, but he could not remember.

It was Anatilda's day until late afternoon when Minor continued his plan. He and Lemuel and Anatilda's youngest brother Buck would ride their horses to Farmerville and spend the night. Minor and Lemuel would catch the first freight wagon of the morning to Monroe, and Buck would bring the horses home. At Monroe they would sign the army papers and ride the train to Madison Parish to join their regiment.

I had plans too. I aimed to look at Minor one more time before he left. Though the Carters would have probably let me use the wagon, I did not ask. As soon as I returned Mrs. Carter's looking glass to her dressing table I started walking to town. When I got close I circled through the woods and came to the Farmerville road just beyond the livery stable. From the hill there I could look down into the village and see anyone coming up the road. I did not know what time they would come or if the arrangements had changed. I sat against a hickory tree and watched a gray hawk with pointed wings and a long black tail. He hunted above the treetops and snatched dragonflies from the air with his feet. It was easy for me to see that in this life he was where he was meant to be.

After a long time a dog barked in town, and I saw many people coming up the road on horseback and in buggies and wagons. They stopped at the livery stable. I ran into the woods and along the road until I got close enough to see the crowd well. Minor and Anatilda were in a buggy with the Claybank mare tied behind. Everyone was happy and laughing. Finally Minor jumped from the buggy and walked around to Anatilda on the other side. He kissed her quickly and spoke to her for long moments. I shut my eyes and strained to hear but mercifully the distance was too great.

Minor mounted the mare and with three other riders came up the road toward me as the crowd cheered them off. They rode two abreast with Minor and Lemuel in front, followed by Buck Tubbs and Mr. Laran. Crouched deep in the brush, I prayed that the horses would not discover me. The soon-to-be soldiers carried bedrolls, mess kits, and haversacks for their personals. The barrels of Lemuel's shotgun and Minor's fine rifle held Cherokee roses bound with love vine. Minor had never looked more splendid. I had seen his brown linsey pants before but never the ruffled silk shirt. He was bareheaded and wore new riding boots with the blunt, silver spurs that quieted the mare. As he rode by he looked straight ahead. With five steps, a span that I later measured, I could have grasped his leg. Instead my eyes were on the saddlebags. They bulged as once before, and though I could not be certain of its image, the corner of a small painted canvas showed clearly in the setting sun. I savored this thought as solace on the walk home—that and the fact that Minor would not be in Anatilda's bed on her wedding night.

When Lemuel limped to our gate a year later bringing grave news of Minor, it was as if I had already imagined the scene and was ready to act. As soon as my first agonies passed I gathered the thoughts that had been sorting in my head during his absence. For a long time I had compared my life to that of the soft, brown spider who rides her drifting strand of silk across miles of autumn sky. We were both on journeys guided by the winds of creation but with one major difference—the spider and her sisters floated to a certain destiny while I seemed only to wander, to remain forever in-between.

The quandary was as basic as the mixed blood flowing in my veins. I was born in-between two races of people. Had I spent my life with one or the other, the passage would be more certain. Growing up in the Indian village of my mother's people and moving to the Carters' was only a physical change. In many ways I had left one place but never arrived at another.

Strangers in passing knew at once I was in-between by the color of my skin. And if I should speak only a few words, even a blind man could tell. It is mostly the words in books that flow into my talk. The books were those chosen by a physician, an artist, and a teacher. Stirred in are simple words of unschooled neighbors and old words of a Choctaw village. I cherish them for their differences, but sometimes I am embarrassed because my words too are in-between.

Appearance and speech betrayed my separateness to everyone. What they could not imagine were the depths of this condition in my mind. Since I came to live with the Carters, my every thought was in-between. Rains had washed a gully in the yellow clay of the poor-land field behind the village dump. The gully was deeper than my head, and once when I tried to hop across, I got stranded with a foot on each side. Though I strained and twisted with all my strength, I could not jump to either edge. Such were my thoughts, always precarious, drawn, never on firm ground. More often than not they tumbled with me into the mud of the gully. This happened every time I thought about my place in the world. Especially, I could not seem to blend the thoughts in my head concerning my relationship to the land. White people, on one hand, see themselves as separate from the land. They say God said to use the earth as they see fit. Choctaw, on the other hand, consider themselves part of the land, a verse in the song of the seasons. My place was in-between, not a blend of the two because they could not be mixed. One foot was on either side. I have been described as reserved or worse, but my silent excuse is the state of my mind, which I have yet to master by willful intent.

I had not known love for a man until I met Minor. My mother had spoken to me of such before I left her village, but I could not grasp her meaning. Then, as I grew up I watched men and women who were said to be in love. But none of them ever acted like those in books. Some even declared their love but treated each other as they did the land—separate from themselves.

My love for Minor, however, flourished over time. It did not bloom only when I was in his arms and fade with his absence. As the months passed he became part of me. The notion grew naturally like woodbine around a tree. Neither his marriage to Anatilda nor the darkness of war created a doubt in this matter. When Lemuel came, the only part of my being that was not in-between was my love. I knew at once that I must go to Minor.

Chapter 5

Preparations for the trip took two days. I told the Carters my intentions at the supper table. I was determined to go with or without their blessing and was surprised when they did not object. They just sat there looking old and sad. Finally Mr. Carter stood up and said to me, "You are a woman now. Your work has more than paid your dues in this house. I would chain you in the corncrib if I thought it would turn your mind around. Go and learn for yourself the futility of your hopes. I only pray that God has mercy on your foolishness."

The tears burst from my eyes and I ran sobbing to hug him and Mrs. Carter for the eight years of their love. "Do not give up on me now," I begged. I clutched Mrs. Carter's hand and said, "You always told me to fill my heart with good words, be they spoken or from the pages of books. I have done so, and now they tell me to act in this way. It is your wisdom that ensures my well-being."

Kneeling between them at the table then I asked two questions. The first was for permission to keep their last name as my own. The second was, "May I borrow Fox for a few days?" They both wrapped their arms around me, and we all three wept for a long time.

Fox was the Carters' name for the mule. I called him Chula, which is the Choctaw word for fox. I heard his story from Minor, who learned it from his mother.

Within a year of their marriage the Carters had a son named Daniel. He was his father's pride and joy. In time he followed Mr. Carter around the farm learning first the simple chores and later the ways of a man's work. When Daniel grew as tall as a certain pine knot in the cabin door, Mr. Carter taught him to plow. He began by teaching his son to dress the harness properly, to mend a torn collar with moss and rawhide, and to tend the ailments of hard-working animals. Soon Daniel no longer had to struggle to keep the plow handles upright. The lines tangled less often, and daydreams mingled with the slice of the plowshare and the smell of earth.

Daniel's favorite mule was a young dun-colored trickster. He earned the name Fox by slipping halters and opening gates to raid the cornfield. He was even known to close a gate behind himself so as not to share stolen larder with other stock.

After a spring day's lessons with his mother, Daniel hitched up the mule for a second pass over a small patch of new ground south of the house. He rode the plow down the lane from the barn to keep the point up until he reached the turn-row. One giant elm, girdled and dying, stood sentinel in the field. He began plowing against the woods and worked toward the lone tree.

Sometime that afternoon a dark cloud sailed in from the West. It was not big enough to be noticed by those working near the house. No rain fell as it crossed over the new ground. I think it was a misery cloud. It sent a bolt of lightning to stop the misery of the suffering tree. As misery cannot be destroyed, it was passed along to Daniel's parents.

Mr. Carter found him when he did not come for supper. Still holding the charred lines he lay dead on the ground. The tree was split in three pieces, and the plow was brittle and useless forever. Fox walked in a circle around them all, stumbling over clods he could not see.

Daniel was buried across the road from the cabin. Mr. Carter marked his grave with a piece of petrified wood until a stone could be cut. Mrs. Carter planted a cedar tree. Minor's mother said they rarely smiled again until after I came to live with them.

Blind Fox never worked again. He learned to walk with a high-stepping gait and grew fat with kind treatment. His raids on the forbidden fields were no less frequent partly because of the Carters' tolerance. Such behavior in another animal would have resulted in a quick bargain for a traveling hostler.

I needed Chula to carry my trappings to Vicksburg and to bring Minor home. Mrs. Carter helped me parch twenty pounds of corn. She gave me jerked beef, dried beans, salt, meal, and a small tin of lard. I gathered clean rags for bandages and a few medicines. Mr. Carter drew a map and wrote names of people who lived along the way. He urged me to take his small two-barreled derringer, but I asked for his large hunting knife instead. We wrapped these things and others in oilcloths and packed them in two canvas bags. When Chula was loaded, he stood very still and listened to our talk.

I left with a small toothache on the second morning after Lemuel came. I went first to Minor's mother to tell her of my plans. She was in bed and covered with quilts on a hot day. Her violoncello lay at her feet without strings. I thought she was having fever chills, but it was the sickness of grief. She insisted that I take thirty dollars in gold coins and gave me a promise note to pay anyone for services rendered to aid her son.

"Abita, fashionable society considers the way I hold the violoncello unladylike," she said. "A host of teachers tried to force me into contortionist positions, but I did not conform. Like the masters I hold it between my knees, and I am proud. You and I are alike in ways. Because we are different from others, people here speak of us as misfits. To avoid their barbs we live our lives in reserve. But they misjudge the sinew in our reticence." Then in a voice that seemed far away she continued. "There is something you must know. Anatilda and Mink left yesterday for Monroe. If the train is not running they plan to follow the track to DeSoto Point and cross the river there to Vicksburg by bribing the Yankees.

I have little faith in her. She is indiscreet and impetuous. You are my true hope, cher."

Mrs. Barrett was still beautiful. Her sorrow could not mask the Creole grace. I kissed her goodbye.

The road north out of town led through the Tubbs' plantation. I stopped for a moment to tighten Chula's girt and hurried on. Field hands were chopping cotton in the distance, and an overseer, maybe one of Anatilda's brothers, sat a horse close to the workers. They paid me no attention.

Mr. Tubbs was away in Texas or Mexico trying to sell his cotton crop. Only one of his sons was gone to the war. Two others were in the home guard, and Buck was too young to enlist. Anatilda was said to rule the roost when her father was absent. I figured Mr. Tubbs' not being home was the only way she got off after Minor.

The road soon began to turn east and dipped down to the l'Outre. The bayou was clear and narrow with a sandy bottom. Sunken logs marked the ford. Chula drank deeply and put his nose against my back. He kept it there as he followed me across, and I felt the warm trust in his breath. After that I did not have to lead him. He stayed close behind, adjusting his pace to mine. Ears always forward when he walked, he never once in many miles stepped on my heels. I could tell that some light passed through his eyes. When a cloud suddenly covered the sun or when we walked into deep shade, he would often stop and tremble with fear until I touched him. Then he would sigh and march on. He traveled as well or better at night.

The hills across the l'Outre gave way to a level, forested plain. The pine trees were different with longer needles and deeper bark. The color of the soil changed from red-orange to rusty yellow and made a deep powder in the track. We continued on through the hot day and saw no other travelers.

In the evening we came to the edge of the Ouachita River bottoms. I chose a campsite out of sight of the road. Chula grazed on broomsedge as I built a small fire and ate supper. The fireflies outnumbered the mosquitoes and coolness settled in. Sleep soon overcame the apprehensions of the first day of my journey.

A log-god hammering on a hollow tree woke me just after first light. In fifteen minutes Chula and I were back on the road. The pine trees stayed behind as we walked into the deep overflow lands a mile west of the river. High water from the spring floods left rings around the pin oaks twenty feet above the ground. Ruts in the sticky, black mud marked the passing of wagons. We began to hear a commotion toward the river.

Alabama Landing is the last steamboat stop in Louisiana. Boats passing on up the Ouachita travel through miles of swamp before reaching the next wood yard in Arkansas. The landing is no more than a cut in the bank made with mule slips. Just upstream the only ford for twenty miles in either direction allows crossings in the summer and fall. Only flatboats can pass up at these times. Settlers from Alabama off-loaded here and crossed in covered wagons to claim what they called "new lands" to the west. They put their old names on the "new country" as they would put salve on blistered feet.

On this morning the river heard the peculiar noises of cows bawling and black men imitating the cussing of white men. The ford was filled with a herd of fine Durham cattle being driven by twenty slaves and three overseers. They let the cattle drink their fill and began to holler them across. The slaves threw rocks to turn the strays and a white man on horseback cracked a long whip to keep them moving. Two loaded wagons followed behind the drovers.

Chula and I stood well away from this racket until the herd passed up the road in the direction we had come. A boy driving the last wagon stopped to adjust a harness as we walked down the cut. He stretched his skinny frame to its tallest notch and spoke to me in a manner of self-importance.

"Morning mam." I guessed his age to be fourteen. His face was round and could not bear another red freckle. "Where ya headed?" he asked.

"East a ways."

"You best not go too far east. The Yankees are a swarmin' all the way to the Macon. We barely got the Durhams and what's left of our field hands out. Half of 'em done run to the Yankees—cattle and niggers both. We're the Scotts from Lake Providence. Lost our plantation last year to Grant's men. We been in Texas ever since. My uncle and me—my uncle and I—we came back to get the field hands from the Macon where we left them with the overseer until we got a good place for 'em."

I thought that if I were a Yankee I would be disappointed in this loyal southern boy because he would volunteer his life history and eliminate a good excuse for torture. He continued to talk as Chula and I waded into the ford.

The bottom east of the river was a good four miles wide. An old hurricane made for slow going. Most of the big trees had been sawed out of the road but it still weaved around upturned clay-roots. We were happy to reach higher ground.

At mid-day the road turned south, and we came upon the biggest prairie I had ever seen. It was narrow but near as long as the river bottoms were wide. Grass grew in clumps the size of a dishpan and taller than my head. I once read a book that said prairies stretch for a thousand miles in the Kansas country. The thought of living in a land without trees made me uncomfortable.

Mr. Carter's map showed Boyd's Ferry on Bayou Bartholomew just beyond Prairie de Butte. A small farm straddled the bayou at the crossing. It looked run down, and I thought no one was around until a shrill, piercing squeal sliced the dreariness of the place. I knew the sound, but Chula balked and would go no farther down the path that led to a half-log barn. In a side pen a man wearing a blood-soaked apron was cuttin' shoats. One at a time he held them upside down between his legs and pared their seeds. With each deafening squeal a giant sow in the barn would charge and crash against the walls.

The man, covered with blood, paid her no mind. When he finished, he suddenly stood up straight and stared at me as though he knew of my presence all along. I did not like his looks. He opened the barn door to turn the sow in with the pigs and walked toward me holding his knife by the blade.

Hoping to stop him before he came closer, I asked, "How much to cross on the ferry, sir?"

He came on and only stopped when I began to back up. He smelled worse than any hog I had ever come across. His eyes were up to no good.

"What's yore name, missy?" he drawled.

"I am Abita…Carter… and if you are the ferryman I would like to cross please."

"Well Miss…Carter, I'm pleased to know ya. Why don't you come in the house and rest a spell. It ain't healthful for a woman to travel in the heat of the day."

"I am sorry, but I must be going. I can manage the ferry myself if you are busy."

He turned the knife around in his hand.

"The ferry ain't runnin'," he said. "The bayou is pert near dry. You kin walk across."

I started to leave and he added, "But it ain't for free."

I was foolish then and felt little fear in this situation. I thought that I could outrun this man. My concern was losing Chula.

"How much?" I asked.

He continued to stare and finally said, "Two bits." He held out his open bloody hand.

I stepped back and pulled the purse from my waistband. Without taking my eyes off him I chose a quarter from amongst the gold coins, put it on a fence post, and retreated to Chula.

"Be seein' ya soon likely enough," he called after me.

In only a few minutes we were across the bayou and passing quickly down the road away from an evil that I could feel. At dusk we neared the village of Bastrop and left the road to find a campsite. We watered at a small stream and camped without a fire. I figure we came fourteen miles on this day.

Sleep would not stay with me in the night, and when the dreams came I wanted no more of it. When I dozed the ferryman pursued me riding the giant sow. With her head to the ground she popped her razor tushes and trailed our evasive path. The man rode cross-legged on her back and whetted the bloody knife. Finally, I sat up against a tree and brushed my hair till dawn.

The village of Bastrop was not much bigger than Iron Branch. The courthouse of Morehouse Parish filled a square surrounded by shops and other business establishments. I bought iodine and Sudlitz powders at the mercantile to add to my medicine bag. From here the Prairie Mer Rouge road was well traveled and ran due east. We walked out of town into the mid-morning sun.

After about two miles we came to the edge of a bluff taller than the trees that grew at its base. In times of great floods the lands below became an ocean as the Mississippi River spilled its banks to cover all but the highest islands. On this day the river was forty-five miles away, and I could see no evidence of recent visits.

The road soon passed into a prairie even larger than the earlier one. Some of the first white men to farm in north Louisiana settled here and called the place Prairie Mer Rouge. A community with that name grew up in the middle of the opening. Mr. Carter bought cottonseed from a man here because the variety was not as prone to stunting on cool nights. Mr. Carter had told me to call on him.

The man's name was Abraham Duckworth. Like most of the landowners here he was called a planter, not a farmer. The difference, the best I have been able to figure, is in the amount of land and slaves a person owns. I reckon you could also catch and measure the volume of sweat that drips from the brow of each and make an educated guess. House size may tell too. I passed several equal to the Tubbs' before I found Larksong.

Thinking on this, I was struck by a skewed similarity. Planters name their houses and plantations. My mother said her people once named the many summer fishing and shelling camps along the waterways. Indians named places in order to know them, while planters declared names as an act of possession.

Mr. Duckworth was not at Larksong. Two spotted bird dogs met me at the gate and barked up a black housemaid. In short order Mrs. Duckworth appeared at the front door with a young man and put the place in motion. She called a Negro boy who led Chula away to the barn, and I was invited in to the shade of the gallery for cool drinks. Mrs. Duckworth's demeanor seemed stiff at first, only the obligatory requirements to deal with the daughter of her husband's customer. She likened to me though when she discovered I knew Mrs. Barrett. They had been friends in New Orleans, and she was curious as to every detail of her life in recent years. I could see some sameness in them, and I told her what I knew.

Age had worn on the elegance of Mrs. Duckworth. She softened the rough edges with genteel manners and fine trappings. A carved ivory clasp bound her gray-streaked hair. She wore a high collared dress trimmed in fraying lace and seemed to float about the house with no visible movement of her joints.

The young man's name was Lieutenant Wiley Rhymes. He was introduced as a cousin and appeared to be the only other white person on the place. He did not resemble Mrs. Duckworth. His build was stocky, his eyes blue, and his straight yellow hair cropped close. His speech was impaired with something akin to a stutter, only it caused him to occasionally drag a word in a sentence. Later I wondered if he slurred his speech in his dreams. He wore a new Confederate officer's uniform with coat sleeves too long for his stumpy arms. When he grasped my hand in introduction, I thought his to be remarkably soft for someone exposed to the rigors of horse soldiering. He said he was on furlough from his cavalry unit posted near Jackson.

I liked them both. Mrs. Duckworth had an appetite for conversation, and Lieutenant Rhymes was a pleasant, obliging companion. In a couple of hours I learned the news of Larksong and Prairie Mer Rouge in general. Mr. Duckworth had left in May to personally offer his services to President Davis. He carried a secret plan that he was sure would entice the French to assist the new republic in a significant way. Soon after, the plantation overseer, described as a barely tolerable misfit, left for parts unknown. Mrs. Duckworth said that she was managing fine though and that most of her eighty-five slaves were loyal and trustworthy. Only seven hundred of the twelve hundred acres were planted because of the war. Twice as much corn as cotton was growing, just the opposite of a normal year. People were starting to have serious worries about food shortages.

In the late afternoon Mrs. Duckworth called a house servant and ordered a decanter of muscat wine and three glasses. I tried to beg off, but Lieutenant Rhymes insisted and I felt it would be rude to argue further. I had never tasted spirits and had no intention of swallowing more than a sip. We sat in wicker chairs on the porch and talked until the heat of the day began to pass. I became anxious to continue on.

Then the dogs stirred again when an oxcart rounded the curve in front of the house. Its solid wooden wheels were painted with alternating red and black triangles. The steer plodded along too slowly to blur the colors. Something about the man hunched in the driver's seat caught my eye and compelled me to cry out almost against my will.

"Who is that person?"

Mrs. Duckworth did not hesitate. "Butcherman," she declared.

"Mam?"

"He's the butcherman from Boyd's Ferry. He travels from plantation to plantation to peddle his slaughtering services. It is said that he can skin and carve a beef into bite-size pieces before most men can jerk the hide off. Mr. Duckworth won't have him on this place. Too peculiar. He says the man has no sweat glands, just like swine. Look at that cloud of flies about him now."

A cold chill ran down my spine, and the goose bumps rose on my arms. In these moments people in my mother's village would say that a 'possum was running across my grave site.

The Lieutenant added, "A few years b-a-a-a-ck, a clan of Irishmen headin' west camped on his place waitin' for the river to go down. Three of their babies just disappeared in the n-i-i-i-ght. Some folks said they all got drunk and the hogs ate the youngins'. Some say the Butcherman had a hand in it 'cause the Irishmen wouldn't pay his thief-high ferry fees."

The cart went out of sight behind the boxwood hedge traveling the only road east.

Mrs. Duckworth poured the last of the wine into Lieutenant Rhymes' glass.

"Miss Carter," she said, "you must stay the night. I'm thoroughly enjoying your company, and besides the hour is late for you to make much progress before dark. The Lieutenant has procured for us a special supper treat. You shouldn't miss it."

A few minutes earlier and this talk would have passed through my head with no effect. The oxcart changed things. Her words made sense, and I agreed to stay, but it made me feel bad in a queer way.

I saw to Chula. He had a stall to himself in a new cypress barn and plenty of fresh water. The hostler said he would feed him a gallon of cracked corn, but I told the man a half-gallon would be enough. I could not risk foundering my mule.

A slave girl named Sarah led me to a bedchamber in the back corner of the L-shaped house. The wealth of this family showed in its chamber pots no less than its marble mantles. I washed and rested until the dinner bell rang.

Only the three of us sat at the long walnut table. Partridge, battered and fried, was the main course. The Lieutenant, at the urging of Mrs. Duckworth, described how he tolled them in, all bobwhites, by whistling their fight call. One by one he shot off their heads with a small-bore rifle as they flew into the yard expecting a rival suitor. They spoke of this as a great feat. In my mother's village ten-year-old boys did the same with cane darts, but I did not tell them.

Later in the parlor the talk was mostly of the nearby war. I pressed for details, and the Lieutenant obliged. All spring Grant had killed his own men and hundreds of runaway slaves by trying to dig canals around Vicksburg on the Louisiana side. The fevers and the river whipped him. In April Admiral Porter ran some boats by the batteries on the bluffs. The Yankees put all their efforts into capturing Vicksburg in order to control all of the Mississippi River. They thought this would break the back of the South.

The Lieutenant said the Confederate army did not have many men in the north part of the state. General Dick Taylor and General Walker from Texas tried to slow the Yankees down with hit-and-run raids. The hottest action was at Milliken's Bend and Lake Providence in early June, but it did not amount to much. The Confederates were always outnumbered ten to one. Pinhook, thirty miles east, was the closest the enemy had been to this place. Now Grant surrounded Vicksburg and laid siege to my destination.

White claret was the drink of the evening for Mrs. Duckworth. The Lieutenant sipped steady from a silver pocket flask. As time passed and drink flowed, they began to talk around me. I soon felt like an obstacle on a path they had abruptly decided to take. When I asked the Lieutenant where he had gotten a two-month-old *Harper's Weekly* published in New York, his glance was sudden and cold. I thanked them for their kindness of the day and retired to the rolling-pin teaster bed.

Chapter 6

In the morning breakfast was served at sunrise. Mrs. Duckworth was fully dressed when I joined her in the dining room. She expressed concern for my well-being and said she wished she could accompany me. I thanked her again and went to the barn for Chula.

The plantation was alive with Negroes preparing for the day's labors. Corn harvest was underway, and the drudgery of the hoe was set aside for a while. A line of wagons filled with women and children passed down the lane toward the fields. Their clothes were faded reds and blues and greens. They shouted and laughed at each other from wagon to wagon. Wheels creaked, traces jingled, and the drivers spoke to the mules in foreign tongues. To me in this moment these people looked happy.

Chula was excited by the commotion he could not see. He swiveled his neck and worked his ears and nose to catch signals for his good senses. I think his knowledge of the goings on was greater than mine.

When we rounded the corner of the house Lieutenant Rhymes with brass field glasses hanging from his neck stood beside a buggy hitched to an old gray roan. Mrs. Duckworth joined me from the gallery and announced that she had good news for my cause.

"Miss Carter, the Lieutenant has volunteered to accompany you as far as the Macon Hills. It will ease my mind to know that you will be safe in his presence to that point at least."

The Lieutenant bowed and dropped his hat. I did not expect this situation.

"Oh mam, I could not possibly accept. Your kindness has been more than I deserve." I spoke this in the direction of the Lieutenant also.

She insisted, "Child, don't argue with me. It's not polite. There are dangers in this world that you can't imagine. Besides, the Lieutenant has promised to return tonight with more fresh game for the pot."

The oxcart rolled through the back of my mind as I unloaded Chula and placed the bags in the buggy box. I tied him behind and climbed aboard with the Lieutenant. A distant treeline marked the boundary of Larksong, and in less than an hour we had left the plantation and the peculiar prairies behind.

The road was beginning to grow up. For years it had been a main passage for settlers from the East and traffic back to the Mississippi River. Three years before, the railroad from DeSoto Point to Monroe had been completed, leaving this route to the saplings of red gums and bitter pecans. It was mostly surveyor straight and easy to follow in spite of the hindrances. The natural gait of the old mare matched Chula's, making progress through the forested tunnel slow but steady.

The Lieutenant dipped macaboy snuff. Ever so often he would spit to the side, and on each occasion he would take a drink from his pocket flask. We talked enough to keep the situation polite, but I did not find him as interesting as the evening before.

He had a beautiful gold Napoleon watch on a long, braided chain. He checked it regularly and the horse was allowed to rest for a few minutes beginning exactly on the hour. I noticed that the initials on the watch were not his and asked if they were those of a relative. He did not answer.

At one place of rest squealer ducks sang their comfort call from the buttonbush thicket of a cypress slough. The Lieutenant decided to stalk them with his rifle. Before he got close enough for a shot the calls changed to low danger whistles, and I knew his efforts were wasted. He squandered a shot anyway as they flushed low and away from harm. He came back muttering about Mrs. Duckworth's demands.

Bayou Bonne Idee was nearly dry and we crossed on a bed of logs. Patches of cane began to appear. The waist-high fronds of palmetto covered the ground so that you could not see your feet if you left the road. In every wet spot I looked for tracks, and as sure as I breathed the signs of an oxcart lay certain before us.

The Lieutenant pulled up in the afternoon and got out of the buggy. He said there was a cabin just ahead. He told me to continue on toward the Boeuf River and said that he was going to hunt for a while and meet me on the road later. I drove on and soon came to a small, poorly tended field with a cabin on the backside. Dogs barked and a stooped-over woman hurried from the garden into the house slamming the heavy door in her wake. Just past the farm I met the Lieutenant standing in the road. He got into the buggy, pulled a new flask from under the seat, and pressed the mare to a fast walk.

We came up on the steep bank of the Boeuf River without warning, the water still and stagnant. If a tall tree were to fall on its shore, it would reach all the way across. I got out and the Lieutenant held the buggy brake hard down the bank. We were lucky. The ferry was on our side and in working order. Few travelers and fewer profits in recent years left the crossing abandoned as a commercial venture. Police juries once auctioned off ferry sites each year to the highest bidder. Competition was keen. That was before the war and before the railroad to the south. Now these Carroll Parish ferries ran by the grace of good Samaritans handy with a hammer and a bailing bucket.

It was no easy task to get the buggy aboard. The deck of the ferry was knee high above the muddy shore in spite of the sloped ends of the boat. I led the mare up close and the Lieutenant laid on her one time with the quirt and a shout. She jumped up on to the deck where I caught her head. He then laid planks from the front of the wheels up to the deck and the horse pulled the buggy aboard. Chula balked at first but I ran a rope behind his back legs and pulled him forward gently. He stumbled onto the ferry and stood there looking indignant as only he could do.

A rope ran from trees on each bank through pulleys at the ends of the boat. Three feet higher another rope stretched between the same two cottonwoods. This was the pull rope. Chula and the mare were moved forward to raise the front of the ferry off the bank. The Lieutenant and I grasped the pull rope on the in-stream end and walked the length of the deck. After several repetitions we were across. The weight was shifted to the rear and the ferry nosed up to the shore. The loading procedure was reversed to disembark. In time we stood atop the east bank and looked down upon the scene of our labors. Up and down the river hard-scaled garfish broke the surface to gulp air in gasps that seemed almost desperate.

The Lieutenant drank and became fidgety as we continued on. He said he had expected to see more game and return to Larksong before now. I assured him that I was quite capable of carrying on alone and encouraged him to head back. At the five o'clock rest break he agreed.

I thanked him and offered to pay for his time. He looked at me for a moment as if considering the offer but begged his leave and wished me luck. When he left, I did feel loneliness but not for him.

The Macon Hills are not really hills at all. This land is more of a flat-topped ridge between Boeuf River and Bayou Macon that rises above the swamps and great floods of the Mississippi River. The forest is not dense, and dark green tops of scattered pine trees pierce the canopy of post oaks and ash. The soil is yellow in the dry, cracked ruts of the road. As high ground the ridge begins in Arkansas and runs south between the rivers to Sicily Island. At my crossing point it was twelve miles wide.

There were few if any planters in the Macon Hills. The farms were hardscrabble, and some outsiders spoke of the people with low words. Mr. Laran once said all Maconites were close kin to each other and the devil with little difference amongst 'em.

I did not see anyone as I left the road to follow a dry creek in search of a campsite. Just beyond, it passed through an opening with thorn trees sprinkled about. A wallow pawed into the streambed by deer and other animals held a small pool of water—enough for the night.

I built a fire and made coals to fry Mrs. Duckworth's salt meat and potatoes. Chula grazed peacefully and followed the shifting smoke of the campfire to avoid the evening flies. I was content when the sun set after a long day and looked forward to the lingering summer twilight before darkness. In these times I gathered courage for the night.

A bullbat appeared suddenly then and began to write a veiled warning in his loops and turns above the wild meadow. Even his buzzing calls I did not interpret, much less heed. Such is the state of sensibilities of one who is in-between.

Chula heard the creaking wheel before me. He raised his head and turned to face the trail. At first I could not be sure it was coming toward our campsite, but it soon became louder and there was no doubt. The heavy wheel of the oxcart cried for grease. Panic is the only word for my emotions. For long moments I stood frozen and listened—to the wheel, to the bullbat, to the drone of the evening's first locust. A glance at Chula broke my trance. He stood calmly, ears forward, breathing as normal—a paradox in a crisis. I dove for the canvas bag and dug frantically for Mr. Carter's long skinning knife.

The man stepped into the opening with a rifle on his shoulder, and against my will I laughed out loud, a hysterical cry of relief. It was not the butcher but Lieutenant Rhymes leading the mare.

I stood up quickly and moved near the fire.

"Lieutenant, I am sorry. I did not expect you."

"Bro-o-o-ke the spindle trying to board the damned ferry." The buggy listed hard to one side. "Closer to Pinhook now than back to Duckworth's. Thought I mi-i-i-ght eat a bite with ya before lookin' up the blacksmith." The whiskey dragged on his burdened words.

"You are welcome to the leftovers. I was going to save them for breakfast but there is plenty for that."

I stoked the fire, wiped out the pan, and went about the business of heating the Lieutenant's supper. My head was light with giddiness. Chula had known. Chula had known the butcher was nowhere about and that our intruder was only the harmless Lieutenant. I should have trusted the little mule.

"Lieutenant, could you pass me the tin of lard next to my pack. We will have fried potatoes in no time."

He reached into the bag and pulled out the daguerreotype of Minor.

"Is this your beau? The one you're going to all this trouble for?" He held the image at arm's length and strained to focus his drink-laden eyes.

"He is my – good friend," I added.

He stared hard at the figure and gently placed it back in the bag.

"The lard is behind the pack," I added.

He picked it up, loosened the lid, and tossed it to me.

"R-u-u-u-b it on your bosom."

"What!?" Surely I did not hear him correctly.

"I said rub the lard on your bosoms."

I could not believe these words were coming from the Lieutenant. They did not fit him any better than the short-sleeved coat.

He stepped over to Chula and patted his neck. "You're real fond of this mule, ain't ya?" He put his rifle barrel against the side of Chula's head and the wickedness came forth. "Do what I t-o-o-le you or

I'll paint the treetops with his brains." He kept stroking Chula's neck. "Do it now!"

The lard was soft from the hot day. I tried to do as he demanded without revealing myself.

"Take off the shirt."

The situation was racing away with me and I could not help it. I turned my back to him, unbuttoned my blouse and watched it fall to the ground.

"Turn around here real sl-o-o-o-w so I can look at ya."

I did as he said. He was breathing as if he had just run a mile.

"Now the skirt and more lard." He said it with his jaws clinched.

Weakness washed over me and I felt that my legs would no longer support me. "I can not," I said.

He shot Chula then. In one motion he cocked the rifle and pulled the trigger. The roar, the flash, and the blood came together. The smoke was an instant later, and from within it he leaped and forced me to the ground. I fell on my back and he lay heavy on me, one hand grasping my hair and the other tearing at my skirt. These thoughts come to me now as though I were another person standing to the side and watching this happen. Such was my consciousness as he struggled to commit his crime. I twisted and rolled but he stayed atop me as I began to drift away. I knew it was inevitable.

From under a palmetto frond the serpent appeared. In my trance she struck in slow motion, gaping her mouth as she passed over me to hit the

Lieutenant full in the face. One fang buried deep in the cheek beneath his eye, and the other curved through the side of his nose and came out again, the venom dripping onto my breast. For a moment the scene was calm and peaceful. The rattlesnake was still and beautiful. Her skin was marked with the velvety hues of ripe peaches and winter sunsets framed in bronze. She hung there quietly. The Lieutenant made throaty, whimpering noises, a sound like nursing puppies. His eyes crossed and uncrossed and rolled back in his head. Finally, he tore the snake away, threw her into the brush and ran moaning in the direction of the road.

The attack stunned me for a long while. I remember little of the night other than that I cleaned myself up and sat against a tree until the gray dawn and my senses returned. When the light came I saw the Lieutenant's horse still harnessed to the buggy. The mare rolled in the dust and trotted off to the west when I set her free.

It took all of my strength to search for Chula. I dreaded the thought of seeing him, but I could not leave without saying goodbye. He had not fallen where he was shot and a blood trail lay north along the dry creek. In places the palmetto looked to have been sprayed with his blood. He had crashed through tangles of vines and fallen often. I imagined his pain and fear. The trail continued on for a quarter mile, and more than once I envisioned a log to be his prostrate form. Just ahead the ground began to rise and a giant mound came into view. I became afraid again, thinking of the spirits of the ancient people who built this monument. I was to the point of running away when I saw Chula. He was standing at the foot of an earthen ramp that led to the top of the mound. It came upon me as a powerful sign.

Though his appearance was frightening, Chula was not mortally wounded. Dried blood coated his head, neck and withers. The shot had passed through both ears cutting a clean hole in one and notching the other near its base. The big vein in each ear was severed and covered with clots. The muzzle blast had singed the side of his head. He stood there patiently as if he were waiting for me to come.

I left him and went back to the campsite to pack my belongings. I stashed most nearby and carried the rest to the mound. The morning passed while I tended Chula with a poultice of mullein and chickweed. By the afternoon he was browsing kunti, jerking the vines from trees, and threatening to start his ears bleeding again.

I felt compelled to climb the mound. It looked to be sixty feet high and was shaped like the top half of a hornet's nest. The sides were steep except for the ramp to the east. Large trees of sassafras, elm, hickory and red oak covered its slopes and peak. The builders of this place were older than the ancestors of these trees. This was revealed in giant logs that rested head down in a slow return to the earth.

Halfway up, a fresh fox den was burrowed into the mound. Pieces of broken clay pots lay scattered in the diggings. I examined them closely for a connection. Some old women in my mother's village still made pots of clay when I was a girl. They mixed the crushed shells of river mussels into the wet mud to give it strength. The shaped vessels were etched with beautiful designs and fired to a polish.

Pots on this mound had no shells to make them strong, and the markings were broad loops and circles within circles. I could not detect a Choctaw presence here. Still, there was something in the essence of this place I could feel but not grasp. I concluded that it might involve the people of my father's mother.

Before I reached the top of the mound, I decided to spend the night there. It was too soon for Chula to travel, and there were issues pressing against the inside of my head. For days I had kept some thoughts imprisoned on the edge of my consciousness. The attack released demons of doubt. A positive power emanated from the mound, and it seemed a good place to confront this enemy.

From the summit it was possible to look out over the forest canopy for miles in every direction. The setting sun illuminated thin, wispy plumes of smoke rising far to the east. They were soon replaced by a climbing piece of moon yellow as butter. I sat with my back against a tree and watched its ascent for most of the night. The Psalmist wrote that there is no danger in the moon, but during this time the beasts came and I cried aloud to the universe.

"Who am I to undertake this journey in search of another woman's husband!? What of my motives? Are they right or wrong?"

The biblical word "covet" haunted me, and I wondered if this was my test as God had tried Moses and his people.

"Is this a measure of *my* judgment?" I wondered aloud.

If so, I thought that I had surely failed. My appraisal of the Lieutenant's character and intentions was evidence enough. As a reflection of the whole endeavor, it did not bode well.

I struggled with these issues and others more basic to my selfish wants for hours. I wondered if Minor was alive, if Anatilda was with him now, and of course if he loved me still. Revelations in the soft, pious calls of a horned owl were beyond my understanding, and sometime before dawn I crawled into the mosquito netting, exhausted, and slept until mid-morning.

A cat squirrel barking at Chula woke me. I was hungry and wished the squirrel battered and fried alongside Mrs. Carter's biscuits. The thought of such a delicious breakfast made me homesick to see the Carters. I ate cold parched corn and hoped they were well.

The night's ordeal answered only one of my questions, that being whether to continue on. I could not do otherwise. My determination was innate, as that of traveling wild geese, and did not rise from rational conclusions, which would have surely sent me home. Besides, I was near the halfway mark; the smoke in the eastern sky must be Vicksburg. As parting advice, Mr. Carter had told me not to cross any footlogs with my hands in my pockets. It was his way of saying "be careful," that many falls in life could be prevented. I resolved to heed his counsel diligently from this point forward.

Except for the worrisome flies, Chula showed no ill effects of his wounds. We returned to the first camp, and I washed him as best I could with the limited water. He seemed eager to proceed and pushed me about as I loaded the pack. We left this baneful place and were soon on the main road heading east again.

My plans were to travel slowly the rest of the day and stop early for the night so as not to stress Chula. This we accomplished without incident except for a brief rainstorm in the evening. We camped off the road as usual and during the night heard dogs barking from the village of Pinhook.

Chapter 7

In the morning we had traveled only a short distance when a soldier stepped from behind a tree and challenged us. I was not certain he was a soldier at that moment because of his dress and weapon. His ragged outfit did not resemble a uniform in the least, and he held a rusty shotgun across his breast. I identified myself and obeyed his order to follow him to the officer of the picket guards.

Pinhook is a small settlement, and the several hundred soldiers camped nearby more than doubled the usual population. The army tents and their breakfast campfires set in a grove of oaks gave the impression of a large, pleasant outing instead of a regiment at war. We stopped before the tent nearest the road, and my escort advised a sergeant that I was not a local girl but had traveled from beyond the Ouachita River. The sergeant was tall with skin like smoked leather. He wore a gray army shirt, buckskin pants, and his high boots were freshly blackened. Old Mexico was in his blood and words. He questioned me about my destination and raised a scarred eyebrow when I told him Vicksburg. Pulling my escort aside the sergeant whispered orders that sent him hurrying into the midst of the camp. The sergeant and I engaged in polite, idle talk until he returned, nodding eagerly. I was asked to follow them at once.

We walked toward the center of the sea of tents. The men lounged about in idleness, eating, playing mumbly-peg, and some sleeping still. This was my first view of an army, and I felt strangely disappointed.

A flagpole marked the commanding officers' quarters, and beneath its banner a group of uniformed men gathered around the tailgate of a wagon. They turned to us as we approached, and a tall, bareheaded man in a gold-trimmed coat came forward.

"Good morning, mam. I am Major Lewis of General Walker's Texas Division. Welcome to our temporary home, such as it is." He spoke slowly.

I searched his eyes for sincerity. They were gray, baggy and unrevealing like his uniform. I stepped forward and took his hand.

"I am Abita Carter from Union Parish."

"Pleased to meet you Miss Carter. I hope the name of your home parish doesn't reflect the sentiments of its residents, especially you." He said this and smiled as if to put me at ease.

"Without a doubt the southern cause has the majority there," I said. I did not say that the margin was small and maintained by otherwise apathetic people who were angry about Yankee-forged deprivations. This was Minor's opinion as he had told me a year earlier, and it seemed true enough. Most of the people I knew did not own slaves. Perhaps they would if they could have afforded them, but no matter, they did not, and they just wanted to be left alone. Until the blockade closed the cotton markets and dried up the source of staple goods, most people in Union Parish just did not care about the war.

"Morning beverages are scarce here abouts but I can offer you a cup of fine well water."

"No, thank you."

"May I ask your route of travel to this point?" His interest was genuine.

"I crossed the Ouachita at Alabama Landing. From Bastrop I walked east to Mer Rouge. The Old State Road brought me here. The roads are quite passable, though some crossings are troublesome." I mentioned this because I thought he was seeking information about the country to assist his maneuvers. He was not.

"Miss Carter, I hope you don't think me forward, but there is an urgent matter with which you may be able to assist us."

I was puzzled by the attention of this powerful man and his subordinates.

"Please?" he asked and taking my arm led me to the wagon. At his signal a soldier dropped the tailgate and jerked away a blanket to reveal a sight that drove me back as sure and sudden as a hard shove. My first thought was that it was the body of a beheaded giant. Hair on top of the stump confounded the deranged image. The soldiers studied my reaction.

Major Lewis spoke after several moments: "I apologize for the shock, but it is very important for us to know if you have information regarding this man."

By then I had sorted out the corpse. It was Lieutenant Rhymes, and he was not headless. The poison had swelled his neck and head to an equal, amazing girth. Features of his face—nose, ears and eyes—disappeared in the engorged tissue.

"We found him near the Boeuf River ferry in this condition. He may have been snakebit," said the Major as he led me back to his tent. "Do you know him?"

"He is Lieutenant Rhymes from a cavalry unit," and I began to tell them what I knew—up to a point. I could not bear to relive the details of the attack much less relate it to strange men. I told them he returned to my camp drunk and threatened me. I said the snake bit him under the buggy as he worked to repair it. I said he ran away then, and I was glad because he scared me. These small lies did not hurt as much as I expected.

Major Lewis was very attentive of my story. When I finished he asked me many questions that I could not answer about Mrs. Duckworth and her husband. Finally, he excused himself to meet with his officers.

When he returned he seemed relieved of a burden. "Miss Carter, you are indeed a fortunate woman. The information you have provided confirms our suspicions about the man you knew as Lieutenant Rhymes. Rhymes was not his real name, nor was he a lieutenant for our cause. He was a traitor, a spy, and a cold-blooded murderer to boot."

A cur gyp, perhaps one that I had heard barking from the last night's camp, reared up on the wagon to smell the ripening body under the blanket.

The Major continued, "It would be improper for me to speak of details, but I can say that we have met with difficulties in our efforts to surprise the enemy in recent weeks. Mr. Simpson, his real name, has been busy watching us from a distance and revealing our movements to Grant. He was a sham of the first degree. Nothing that you knew of him was real, even his manner of speech. Like you, most of his acquaintances were naïve as to their danger. Some lost their lives in such innocence. A man was killed and his wife ravaged by this devil in the past month. You passed their cabin on your journey. As for the Duckworths, they are far from being "hot seceshes," and I strongly advise that you avoid any future contact with them at all costs. The situation should become obvious to you."

My thoughts slowed and bogged in the mire of his words.

"I've heard of your mission and destination," he continued. "It is as foolish as it is noble. The enemy controls all points between here and Vicksburg. From what I've seen, accommodating southern ladies is not a high priority of theirs. I would have you escorted home, but something tells me that once abandoned you would be back here in

Carroll Parish before my soldiers." He had begun to scold me like a wayward daughter. "You were obviously not deterred by your recent danger and will not likely change your mind now. Am I correct?"

"Sir, the bodily dangers that I face now are only heat gnats as to the demons I will encounter forever if I quit this calling."

"As I suspected. This calling of yours resembles love." He suddenly seemed tired. "I must detain you for a short while, but I won't send you back. The sergeant will see to your needs. God bless you Miss Carter."

Between them, Gertie and Walter Sawyer did not have one hair on their heads. Both were in their eighties and lived on the edge of Pinhook in a ramshackle log house fast returning to earth. The sergeant made arrangements for me to stay with them and gave specific instructions that I was not to depart for two days. I did not obey this order.

The Sawyers seemed happy to have me and put me up in a small room last used by an Irish field hand rumored to have since been killed at Shiloh. They showed me month-old bullet holes in the cabin and told of how Major Lewis' men repelled a group of Yankee raiders here. Of this event Mrs. Sawyer was more concerned about her trampled chick roses than the death-bearing lead.

Before sunrise the next day I awoke with the strange feeling that I was in the presence of many people. A fife played outside and the smell of fresh dust seeped through cracks in the walls. The room had no window, so I lay still on the cornshuck mattress straining to hear. The fife passed and was followed by the footfall of horses for a long while. When I heard Mrs. Sawyer stirring to build a fire in the patent stove, I got up and she confirmed my suspicions. The soldiers were riding toward Lake Providence with mischief on their minds.

By mid-morning I could wait no longer. Mr. Carter would have said my patience well ran dry. The shawl of my blind faith had begun to unravel, and I needed to know basic things about Minor, the most fundamental of which was—is he alive or dead? Affairs of the heart unconsciously slipped behind these foremost thoughts. Waiting was not an option for me.

I left a dollar on my pillar for board and brought Chula around from the lot to load. The Sawyers did not protest my leaving and gave me two small yellow-meated melons, sole survivors of thieving soldiers. Our parting came after mutual questions.

I asked, "Have you seen a stranger driving a painted oxcart pass through lately? He may be a butcher by trade."

"Passed through a couple days ago," said Mr. Sawyer. "He ain't a total stranger in these parts, the butcherman ain't. Tried to do some work for the soldiers, but they done et up everthang with a hide on it 'round here. Kep on goin'. Always heared he had kinfolks down in Tensas Parish. Can't figure why they would claim him though."

I did not have a ready answer for Mrs. Sawyer's question, "You mostly injun, ain't you girl? You shore don't talk like one, but you got the marks. You mostly injun, ain't ya?"

Bayou Macon was the last big stream between the Ouachita and the Mississippi. It bordered on the east edge of the Macon Ridge as did Boeuf River on the west and resembled it, steep banked and slow. The crossing just beyond Pinhook was known as Lane's Ferry. The ferry was gone, and in its place the soldiers had laid connected wagon beds covered with planks. A sturdy bridge resulted that would last until the winter floods.

Chula and I crossed leaving behind the details on Mr. Carter's map. He was unfamiliar with the country before us, having traveled overland to and from Vicksburg only along the railroad route from Monroe. Mr. Sawyer said it was nine miles from the ferry to the bank of Lake Providence. I expected to travel this distance easily before nightfall.

About five miles east of the bayou, the trail of the Texas soldiers abruptly turned south onto a dim track. Later the forest gave way to cotton fields larger than I could have imagined. In some directions they stretched to the horizon, broken only by the occasional mule tree. Most were unplanted and still bore skeleton stalks of previous years' crops. I wondered then where the vast numbers of people required to till these fields were now. Within days I learned that hundreds awaited the rapture, not laboring with hoes and hope but in the halcyon rest of shallow and hurried graves nearby.

The toothache that I brought from Union Parish got worse. An eyetooth on the left side, it drawed my face. I searched in vain for a toothache tree and the deadening effects of its inner bark. A powder did not give relief, and I began to suffer. Only the drastic change in scenery kept me diverted.

The road ran to the edge of the lake where the great houses once stood and turned hard south to follow its shore. Lake Providence was a blue-green gem surrounded by moss-draped cypress sentinels. It was a mile wide and flowed out of sight in quarter moon curves to the northeast and southeast. I suspected that one or both of the horns had intercourse with the Mississippi. On this late afternoon, patches of sunlight jewels scurried across the surface on either side of passing clouds. Other people were enjoying the lake too. I saw them at a distance fishing from skiffs and along the bank. Most were black, but some were white and unmistakably dressed in blue uniforms.

The first three houses facing the lake were burned. Avenues lined with oaks and blooming magnolias led to chimneys standing watch over cold ashes. Those trees that were too close, the ones that were most loved for their shade and fragrance, died with the mansions though they remained upright and scorched. Many of the plantation outbuildings were not disturbed. Carriage houses, loom houses, barns, cribs and sheds escaped the brand as did rows of slave cabins in the back. The destruction was not fresh and seemed to be months old. Kitchen gardens were fallow, fruit trees untended, and most queerly, there was not a domestic animal to be seen—no mules for the score of plows, no chickens for the master's Sunday dinner, not a bare-ribbed terrier to entertain a pickaninny. A wild turtledove did call softly from the boughs of a tall sweet pecan, and this irony did not pass me by.

The pain lugged my legs in the lengthening shadows. Smoke rose from the far side of the next field, one thick black column that perplexed me and many gray wisps that were surely Yankee campfires. In my condition I wanted to see no one and after watering in the lake sought refuge for the night in a cottonseed shed. It was a two-story of sorts. The bottom served as a drive-through wagon garage and the top stored seeds for the next year's crop. It was nearly empty. From the looks of the destruction thereabouts I doubted that the owner had any kind of earthly future, much less a future crop. I let Chula graze until dark and penned him underneath with rails and a wagon tongue before climbing up to the seed room. I could not eat and slept only after taking a quarter gram of opium.

By the next forenoon the pain was almost unbearable again and my eye swelled shut. Still I decided to take no more of Minor's medicines and trudged on down the lake road. The lazy black smoke of the previous evening rose from a small one-stacked steamer tied at the mouth of a wide ditch. Deck hands paid us no mind as we waded across on a corduroy road. In the fog of my misery I reckoned this to be part of Grant's canal projects. If so, a pirogue would have trouble passing on this day.

The Union camp soon lay just ahead. I climbed down the bank to the lake to wash my face and make a plan. Turtles plunked from a log. Their heads soon reappeared above the surface to stare at the intruder. I reckon they never before saw as pitiful a sight as me.

The cool water on my head gave me relief, and I rested until a commotion began. A barrel hoop suddenly rolled over the bank and into the lake, passing no more than two steps from me. Behind it came a running, caterwauling boy waving a stick wildly. He too rolled into the lake. The water did not affect him. He splashed and probed and performed shallow dives and submerged handstands until at last the hoop was in his possession once more. Triumphant, he waded ashore only to discover a cyclops watching his every move. I cannot describe his expression when he saw me. After long moments of locked eyes I laughed. I laughed out loud and could not stop. The mood swept over the boy. He giggled, stoically at first, but quickly surrendered to peals of delight. Drowning in our glee we pointed at each other, stumbled about, and howled as actors in a hyena comedy. He slapped the water, and I leaned on Chula for support. Finally, we used up our breath and came to our senses.

"What's your name?" I asked the boy.

"Jesse," he said. He looked to be ten or eleven years old, and because of his haircut reminded me of a picture of a monk I once saw in a book. His eyes sparkled a blue brighter than the sky and the lake.

"Well, Jesse, you chased away my troubles for the moment. Do you live around here?"

"We're stayin' at the Richwood plantation house now. We'll probly be movin' on purty soon though. Mam, what happened to yer face?"

"I have a bad tooth, Jesse. If it does not come out soon it's gonna wear me away."

"Why don't ya pull it?"

"I cannot. It's an old one with roots grown deep down in the jawbone. I need help."

The boy stared at me, and I saw when the idea came to him.

"There's a doctor stayin' with my ma. He can get that tooth out!"

He dripped up the bank to the road, and I followed him. I would have followed the devil himself right then if he would have promised to take this tooth he loaned me.

Chapter 8

Within minutes we were in the Yankee camp. It struck me that only two days earlier I had walked into the midst of a southern camp and now I was trodding among their deadly enemy, all men who if dressed in a common uniform would be inseparable. I figured that in order to kill and plunder their own kind as they did, their hearts must be choked with hate. I wondered if they hated each other or the worldly situation. I hoped it was the situation. It made the war easier to understand.

There did not seem to be as many soldiers here as in the southern camp, and those present were more scattered about. Signs were everywhere though of a great army freshly departed. The plantation was grazed clean from the bare, trampled ground to the height the tallest horse could reach on the trees. Thousands of fire rings charred the fields, and only post-holes remained as clues of fences burned to warm suppers and moods.

"I'm glad Pa's gone," the boy said. "He'd whup me fer sure fer jumpin' in the lake." He rolled the barrel hoop along with the stick as we walked.

Once he rolled it between Chula's legs, darting under his lead rope to keep it going. It almost set me to laughing again when I realized that before this morning I had not laughed in many months.

"Where is your pa?" I asked.

"He's spectin' the men down south," he replied.

We came to the Richwood plantation house, which was not burned and was so new that the war had halted its construction. It was rectangular and supported by square, brick columns. The ground level was open all around to park buggies out of the weather. Wide brick steps led up to the first-floor gallery. These shaded porches wrapped around all sides of this level and the unfinished one above. Giant cypress cisterns, painted forest green like the house, stood on legs at each corner to catch rainwater from the roof. The house sat on the high bank back from the lake and spoke of wealth I could not imagine.

I followed the boy to the back of the house and watched as he washed his face and combed his hair at a basin carved into a large rock.

"Do you know what this is?" the boy asked as he pointed down at the brick path between the big house and the kitchen. I shook my head. "Them rebels call it the whistle walk. Ya know why?" I did not know. "They made the slaves whistle when they toted food from the kitchen to the house. Ya know why?"

"No, but you are stirring my curiosity," I told him.

"Well, the master made 'em whistle so he could hear 'em comin' and they wouldn't catch him kissin' on his wife. And somethin' else—the slaves couldn't be tastin' his food while they were totin' it if they wuz whistling.'"

"He must be a pretty smart man," I said.

"Smarter than some I reckon cause he's mostly a Union man. The slaves are free now. They're servants. We don't make 'em whistle."

He led me up back steps, down a hall, and into a room where two women sat in stuffed chairs knitting socks. A little girl played with dolls on the floor. The boy marched in with me on his heels and stood holding his wet cap before the older woman. He started to speak, "Ma—" but she cut him off with a glare that would melt candle wax.

"Lizzy," she called in a not unpleasant voice that gave me some respite, "May we have more light?"

A black girl I had not seen stepped from the corner and opened a tall, narrow window that reached to the ceiling. When she threw back the shutters, the brightness poured in to paint the boy and me in a shaft of radiance that stopped at the woman's feet. She looked us over.

After some moments the boy tried again, "Ma, she needs the doctor. Just look at her face."

"Jesse, please be presentable for the noon meal." The boy took this as his cue and, still dripping on the fancy carpets, hurried from the room.

I would have been less forward and more embarrassed but for my condition. For days events seemed to sweep me along like bay leaves in the l'Outre's autumn currents. The channel had become sinuous, and I could not see around the bends.

"I am sorry, mam. Your son tells me of a doctor here. I have a bad tooth." So I told them of my mission, and they listened with kindness and interest. When I finished, the older lady spoke again.

"Perhaps we can help. Lizzie, will you run for Captain Waters? He is very likely at the peach trees behind the kitchen."

As the black girl raced away, I realized that I had not introduced myself properly.

"My name is Abita Carter."

The ladies stood and shook my hand in turn.

"I am Julia Grant and this is my friend, Mrs. Cummings."

The beckoned Captain Waters entered the room with a basket of fresh peaches. His elegant silver mustache drooped on one side, revealing that he had savored at least some of the juicy offerings placed before the ladies. His impish smile froze when he looked at me squarely.

"Good Lord!" he cried.

Mrs. Grant spoke, "Captain Waters, being one of the finest surgeons in the army of this great nation, do you think you can offer relief to Miss Carter in her terrible predicament?"

The doctor placed gold-rimmed spectacles on the end of his nose and reared back his head. "A foul tooth, I presume?" His accent was heavy with the old English talk. I nodded. He bowed to the ladies and hurried away calling orders to soldiers stationed at the front door. One of them soon came back for me.

The operating theater was under the house. A high-backed rocking chair was leaned back against a long table used to clean vegetables and chickens. The surgeon's instruments were spread on the table amongst butterbean hulls and feathers. His assistants stood on either side of the chair at near attention. They helped me onto this throne and put a pillow under my head.

Captain Waters spoke solemnly, "Miss Carter, I pray that you are able to reach deep into your essence for courage. The procedure is trying but mercifully short in most instances." With that, one soldier held my shoulder and the other lifted high a carriage lamp for light. "Splitter, please," said the doctor.

I tried to leave my body in the rocking chair and go to my mother in her village. Rising in the air and floating above the treetops was easy for me. I did so at will in my dreams. On this day I could not rise higher than the dirt dobber nests on the floor joists above the chair. I kept bumping my sore head, and it hurt dreadfully.

That night I slept on a pallet in the kitchen. Mrs. Grant looked in on me twice and gave orders to the cook to call at once if my situation declined. By morning I felt a new person and resolved never to forget the lesson that good health is seldom appreciated until suffering begins. I thought again of Minor and his health.

After breakfast Jesse came with the message that Mrs. Grant wished to see me if I felt able. I went at once and found her in the same room as the day before, still knitting socks.

"Good morning, Miss Carter. I must say you look much improved this morning."

"You cannot imagine my relief, mam. I am forever thankful of your kindness."

"I have something else that may ease your travels." She handed me a folded slip of paper that smelled of cigar smoke. "It is a pass authorized by my husband. He returned late last night and I told him of your plight. He said it's the least he can do for another player in this terrible drama. He left again early this morning before I could wish him Godspeed." I saw in her then a loneliness that position could not overcome.

"Please tell him of my gratitude. I wish you both peace and happiness."

I left to gather my belongings and read the pass. It was dated July1, 1863, and stated, "Pass Bearer, Miss Abita Carter, through the lines of the U.S. Army to DeSoto Point and beyond, this pass is good for seven (7) days from this date. By command of General U.S. Grant." I felt the currents pulling me again in the direction that I needed to go.

Someone had fed Chula a tub of watermelon rinds and he was happy. We walked south down the road from Richwood and passed many Yankee soldiers and Negroes. The soldiers were going to and fro as on unhurried details while the Negroes were idle or wandering without purpose. In these black people and others that I encountered in days to come, there was a sense of unknown expectations. They stood at the starting line of a great race with promises of a wonderful prize at the end, but no one would fire the shot to send them forward. And no one would point out which of the many paths led straight away from bondage to happiness. There was a difference in these people and the ones I saw at Larksong who had not tasted freedom. The difference confused me.

Soon the levee came to run alongside the road. We climbed to the top to see the great Mississippi River, but it was across a field hidden by willow trees and cottonwoods. The levee was hard packed from traffic and littered with camp refuse. It was the only high ground during the spring flood. That is why the graves were there too—dozens of them marked by low mounds, some with simple wooden Christian crosses—all of them fresh. I learned that mostly Negroes were in the graves with a sprinklin' of Yankees. They were dead of typhus or smallpox. Some of the freed slaves were just worked to death. The road was a better place to walk.

Fallow cotton fields lay flat like a heavy brown blanket on the front lands. Single mule trees offered shade at some point in a half circle on the north side during all of the summer day. The forest began way in the back after the ground dropped away. In some places a plow could run straight for a mile between turn-rows at the road and the swamp. We walked on past more plantations. Some of the houses were burned and some were mostly left alone. At one of these we stopped in the heat of the late afternoon, but only for a moment to water and inquire of Yankee soldiers about the road ahead. Their answer convinced me that we still had a day's travel to the Point, fifteen miles beyond Milliken's Bend, now in sight across a field. We skirted the village before I chose a campsite off the road on the edge of a canebrake. It came to me that the steady rumble to the south that my mind had unconsciously recognized as thunder was not. I fell asleep wondering if a cannon's roar could be a siren's call.

In the morning I witnessed a frightful battle. Chula's stirring woke me at first light. I sat up to see the dust of a great number of horses passing across the field. The rebel colors floated above the dust leading the soldiers straight to Milliken's Bend. The cloud began to jingle as the horses advanced to a stiff trot. Suddenly they stopped. A deep slave ditch ran from the end of the canebrake across the path of General Walker's cavalry to a slough near the road. I do not know if the officers knew of this obstacle, but they quickly turned it to their favor. Crossings were found and all passed except for a hundred who stayed behind. These dismounted, tied their horses in our canebrake, and jumped into the ditch to form a line of defense.

Unknown to me, a great number of Yankees were camped on the river side of the village. Their still-drowsy camp was the target of the raiders. A single rifle shot rang out, and its echo faded into silence. In another time this would have been a sign that Mr. Carter would soon return with squirrels for breakfast. This day it was a delayed trip wire to release piercing animal screams of attackers as they fell on their enemy. After the first volley, gunfire rippled about the camp like innocent fireworks. I could not see the fight because of the distance, but the sounds made my flesh crawl for long minutes. The men in the ditch before me stood to their posts and stared ahead. They felt the change first and pointed to black columns of smoke approaching from upriver. A cannon's roar left no doubt as to the origin of the smoke. By chance or design a gunboat was close when the battle began and wasted no time in coming to the fight. With her first shot, men in gray came riding hard back in our direction from the village. They called to the men in the ditch to be vigilant. Soon all of the Confederate force were in retreat to the cover of the ditch and canebrake. Officers raced about giving orders. The soldiers dismounted and led their horses, three to a holder, to the cane with the others. The commotion waned then but not the tension. I was close enough to hear the high-pitched strain in their voices. Many were panting like dogs from the terror.

All of a sudden I became conscious of my being. We were in a shaded pocket of cane no more than sixty yards from the closest point of the ditch. Horses nickered and their holders cursed in the thicket behind. I hitched the lead rope to Chula's halter and stood close by him. No one had seen us yet. To move would have brought discovery, so we waited like the others.

The Yankees came out of the village in a broad front. A few were on horseback and held sabers high in the early morning sun. Infantry men followed, many more than the Texas soldiers. The blue wave crossed the field quickly with little noise. Not a shot was fired as they came on. When it seemed they would fall into the ditch, a long cane pole with the rebel battle flag atop swept upward from the moat. The volley that followed wilted the Yankee line like scalding water on clover. Those behind hesitated and looked back over their shoulders. I thought they would turn and run away, but a group of their comrades came around the ditch at the road and attacked the Texans on their side. The Yankees in front were encouraged by the move and came forward again. Soon they were all entangled about the ditch. Men grappled and clubbed and slashed. They made noises far removed from civilized men. Some of the Confederates ran for their horses. One jumped from the ditch and tried to sound a bugle. He blew three notes and fell back into what likely became his grave. An overwhelming enemy was smothering the gray-clad raiders.

The gunboat broke up the battle and nearly killed us all. She had been silent since the first shot in the village. Without warning a shell fell from the sky into the midst of the savagery. Others followed quickly, reaping men of both sides without prejudice. Never have I observed such chaos as soldiers struggled to free themselves of close combat and get away from the invisible, whistling death. When a shell fell between me and the ditch, I pulled Chula into the cane and found a small opening where a giant oak had fallen. A boy stood at one edge holding three horses. Before my eyes an explosion swallowed them, the air cleared, and the boy still stood holding three horses—but they were dead, their bodies shielding him from the blast. I tried to force our way into the cane on the far side, but it was too thick. In desperation I led Chula to the log and threw half hitches around a front and hind leg. I jerked them together and pushed him sideways with all my strength. He fell with a grunt against the log. We lay there for a long time.

Guns on the war boat hushed. The soldiers had stopped firing long before her last shot. The morning became hot, and I was thirsty. I was afraid that Chula would twist a gut and die if I did not let him get up. When we could bear it no longer, we came out from behind the log. No one was in sight. We slipped back to our campsite at the field's edge and saw the parings of battle. The sour smell of gunpowder lingered about and gave me a terrible ache deep inside my head. Ambulances were carrying off the wounded Yankees. A guard stood by bodies lined up beyond the ditch. Maybe there were twenty or thirty, all in blue uniforms. I could not see a live Texan on the field. The rebels had disappeared with their injured but left eleven men where they last took a breath. I gathered my belongings, loaded Chula, and headed west. A final memory of this place still firm in my mind is of a butcherbird impaling a lizard on a locust thorn. The thorn was on a cannon-shattered tree lying across a Confederate soldier.

We walked west along the canebrake until it sank into the field. The field yielded to the stark wall of the swamp, and we turned south again along its edge. No one saw us, or if they did they ignored us. Late in the day white and blue cranes and egrets began to fly from all directions into the swamp ahead of us. I suspected they were going to roost over water, so we followed them. Chula smelled it then and pulled me to the edge of a small, muddy pond surrounded by button-willows. The surface was covered with a mat of duckweed. Chula plunged into the shallows and sucked in the hot water, weeds and all. When he was filled to satisfaction, he backed straight out and turned to face me. With an emerald green muzzle, coal black mud to his knees, and a bullet hole in each ear, he shamed the court jesters in Dr. Barrett's books. He also lifted my spirits on a cheerless day.

I found a trickle of running water at the pond's outlet opposite the bird roost and strained it through a handkerchief into my pot. Mosquitoes drove us back to the field edge for the night's camp. I put beans to soak, laid a fire, and watched the shadows grow across the field while Chula grazed. On this evening I came to a decision. The Mississippi River crossing and Vicksburg loomed just ahead. I sensed pending trials that would tax my will, so I decided to abandon Chula and face them alone during this piece of my journey. Tomorrow I would search for a worthy keeper of my faithful companion.

Cannon rumbled through the night. The noise seemed to swell from the exact point of sunrise on the horizon. We watered again with the waking, squawking birds and started for the source of the conflict.

DeSoto Point jutted into the path of the Mississippi River and forced it east against the bluffs at Vicksburg. The railroad met the river at this place. Before the Yankees came, trains had brought beef and produce from Texas to the Point where this freight was loaded onto a ferry for the crossing. Once across, cars of another railroad had carried the precious goods to hungry Confederate armies across the South. Now the army in Vicksburg tasted only famine.

I found the man to keep Chula under a burned-out trestle just west of the Point. He was living with a half grown boy there in a hut made with bridge timbers and pieces of a wrecked boxcar. Guinea hens cackled an alarm as we came up, and a goat jumped on top of the hut. The boy came out a carpet-flap door followed by a black man bare to the waist and barefoot like most. He stooped to pass through the threshold and stood tall and elegant like an African king. So startling was his appearance that I stepped back. The staff he held became a lion spear and the rags he wore a skirt of zebra hide. It seemed a long time before I could utter a word.

"My name is Abita Carter. I need someone to look after my mule while I see to a friend." They stared and did not say a word. The man was the tallest person I had ever seen. "I can pay for your troubles." The boy looked up at the man and after a while the man nodded.

"I am expecting you to take good care of him. He is blind," I said.

The man stepped back into the hut and returned with a kitten that he clutched to his breast and gently stroked with long fingers. Then the boy spoke, "Atlas cain't talk. He ain't got nary tongue. Dem drunk Yankees done cut it out wid de 'smiff tongs. Dem drunk Yankees tell Atlas to say bad words 'bout the Massa. Atlas cain't tell 'em 'cause he love Massa."

At that moment the matter of slavery, which had been absent from my daily thoughts, came forward tangled in irony. I remembered a sermon about white souls and black souls. I brooded about my own and wondered its color.

The boy's name was Quint. Old Atlas used throat noises and arm waving to pass his thoughts to us. His motions went past me, but the boy caught them and said that they would hide and tend Chula as best they could. Atlas walked to Chula's side and made a humming, clicking sound. He offered him the back of his hand to smell and rubbed him in his favorite place under his jaw. I had never known another mule or horse that liked to be rubbed there, and I was surprised that Atlas could perceive this. It eased my worries about leaving Chula.

One of the canvas packs held the medicines and bare vitals I figured necessary until I could return. I left the rest and two gold dollars with Chula's keepers. The Point was just a short distance down the train track, and I soon came again into the stirrings of an army camp.

A single picket guard on the road passed the time tossing a knife at a stump and paid me no mind as I walked by on the track. The place was a supply depot. Wagons loaded with goods were organized in groups with lanes between them. Barrels were stacked in piles amongst the wagons. From my vantage point up on the track it all looked like a game board maze.

Resting flags marked the Yankee headquarters. I spoke to a corporal carrying a journal. "My name is Abita Carter. Can you take me to the officer in charge?"

He seemed puzzled and stared me over. "The colonel is very busy—too busy to address your complaints today." His manner of speech was like the Sanhedrins'.

"I have no complaints sir. I wish to cross the river." I handed him my pass from General Grant. His eyebrows rose even higher when he read it, and he scurried away stopping to look back over his shoulder at me. I could not resist a small, coy wave that sent him into agitated motion once more.

I waited a long time. Many soldiers came and went in the headquarters area. I had begun to think that my pass was gone forever when the corporal finally returned.

"The colonel suggests that you return in the morning. There may an opportunity for civilians to cross then." His manners were now pleasant. "There can be no guarantees but recent developments are promising. We have just received word that the infidels will surrender tomorrow." He looked across the river at the towering bluffs. "What better way to celebrate the birth of our nation!"

The day was the third of July 1863.

Chapter 9

I learned these things from Mink.

Anatilda and Mink had left for Minor in a jump-seat buggy the day before Chula and me, as Mrs. Barrett had spoken. Their plans were to follow the railroad tracks to DeSoto Point for the crossing. These plans flew away as soon as they arrived in Monroe. They learned that the road along the tracks was still wet from the floods and that travel by buggy along this route was impossible. They went to the stationmaster and, as expected, were told that passenger service did not exist. Here Anatilda pitched a fit and seeing a locomotive there demanded that it be stoked especially for her. She declared her privileged status, saying her father owned stock in the railroad. The officer in charge explained that the Yankees had burned some bridges to the east and they were awaiting timbers to mend the damage. Anatilda said that she would wait also and when the repair train left she would be on it. She was, too.

That evening her money found a room in the hotel filled with refugees. She sent Mink back to Iron Branch the next day with directions to fetch another slave to return the buggy to the plantation and special orders to retrieve her forgotten bonnet and parasol. She stayed in the hotel for nearly a week, fussing at anyone who would listen about her chances of catching the itch in this place and spending her time at a prominent table on the shaded veranda. When Mink got back he tended her, slept in the livery stable, and watched her practice baiting man-traps.

Finally enough timbers were gathered to fill two flatcars. These, a coach for the work crew and the new engine, *John Ray,* made up the train. Anatilda and Mink boarded along with three Confederate scouts. All of them left under a cloud of worry because many said that a train is easy to capture, and rumors put Yankees behind every tree.

The engineer was cautious, and the train crawled along. He hoped to see such dangers as a twisted rail or a tie on the track in time to stop. All the bridges were inspected before crossing. The train passed Lafourche Swamp and Boeuf River without incident. On the Macon Ridge a small bridge over a creek had been partly torn down. The workers started repairing it directly but did not finish before dark. The engineer considered going back to Monroe, but Anatilda's impatient words convinced him to stay the night there.

By mid-morning of the next day the repairs were completed, and they traveled on to Delhi and bad news. They learned that Yankee cavalry had razed the Bayou Macon trestle to the waterline the week before and that it would take weeks to rebuild.

The engineer was relieved to know that he could not approach any closer to the enemy. He ordered the timbers unloaded and took on water. Anatilda and Mink stood on the platform and watched as the train backed away toward Monroe. Mink said the engineer was too scared to blow the leave whistle.

The Rebel scouts stayed too, and someone told them of a handcar on the tracks beyond the wrecked bridge. Anatilda heard them arguing about continuing on. One of the boys said he had joined the army just to get a daily cup of coffee, and now that that was gone he damned sure did not want to leak because of a Yankee bullet hole if he ever got another cupful. He said he was not going and walked away. Anatilda jumped right in and told them that she was going. The other two scouts did not stand a chance against her, especially when she told them Mink would do most of the pumpin'.

They found the handcar and were soon underway. Anatilda sat upon her basswood steamer trunk with her parasol and sang time to Mink and one of the scouts as they leaned over the push handles. She declared herself captain of the ship and issued orders to all aboard. Mink said she behaved as if she were on a Sunday afternoon lark instead of a mission to rescue her mortally wounded husband.

In time they came to the trestle over the Tensas River and passed with some difficulty. Danger caught them at the next sharp curve. As they rolled along, the chief scout sat on the front of the handcar with his legs dangling between the rails when suddenly he leaped up like a jack-in-the-box.

Another handcar came around the bend toward them closing hard. Brakes were set on both cars. Each party struggled to identify the other. The handcars coasted now, eyes strained, and the distance became smaller. The Confederates recognized the two Yankees at the same time and reached for their rifles. One of the scouts fired. The Yankees ducked and returned fire. The moving targets spared everyone. All was frantic then. A scout abandoned ship. The other three soldiers reloaded in a maddened frenzy. Anatilda screamed and dug in her trunk. Mink knelt and prayed. The Yankees took aim on the tempest. The final Rebel broke his ramrod in desperation, lost his nerve, and ran away too. Anatilda slammed the lid of her trunk in disgust at not finding a suitable flag of truce. The Yankees hesitated and stared in disbelief as the woman before them stood, pulled off her white silk drawers and waved them in surrender. The handcars coasted to a stop ten yards apart. To say that Anatilda and Mink were captured would not be true. After another brief, bloodless skirmish the Yankees were captives of her tongue, escorting them on to the Point.

Her efforts to cross the river were no more successful than mine. Like me she was told of a chance to cross the following morning. On this night I slept on the riverbank between brush piles ready to be fired by the Yankees if the Vicksburg garrison tried to escape to the west under cover of darkness. A half-mile away Anatilda shamed a quartermaster until he gave up his wagon.

The next morning was the fourth of July. I felt lucky because of the number and because of the strange night before. Boats passed on the river all night, but the cannons remained silent. Soldiers in the Yankee camp shot fireworks into the dark sky, and the general scene was one of much activity and anticipation. I slept poorly and, wet from the heavy dew, rose two hours before dawn to tend overdue spiritual matters.

Between my campsite and the Yankees', a small country church surrounded by cotton fields sat back from the road. Two giant cedars leaning over the path to the front door held their shadows close in the darkness when I went in to pray. To me, a place such as this petitions silence as a term of entry, and I trod lightly on the wooden steps to muffle their creaks. The door was ajar. I stepped into the sanctuary, seeing only as Chula did, and knew at once that I was not alone. A loud rapping noise rising from the altar froze me in place and launched my prayers prematurely. Though lacking thoughtful preparation, my appeals suffered not for gravity. In answer, the rapping stopped. I stepped forward and submitted a "hello" with propped-up boldness to the blackness. The clatter returned but quit abruptly when I halted. I moved, the racket commenced—I stopped, silence again. A force from Heaven pushed me then, shoved my shoulder blades, drove my legs on to the altar and the now wildly drumming clamor. I felt the letters carved into the front of the table— This Do In Remembrance Of Me. Hairy paws clutched my breasts. I cried for holy mercy and fell to my knees. Encouraged by my moans, the beast licked my neck and face as his tail thrashed a cadence on the altar leg.

The grayness of first light spilled through the open door to divulge a redbone hound overjoyed with his new-found company. In spite of the fright, I regained my senses after a while. If the Lord looked down on me during my requests, He was treated with a mighty peculiar sight. He likely does not get many opportunities to see a half-Indian girl sitting in a deacon's chair, scratchin' the ears of a half-starved dog, and praying for all she's worth. God's lesson that morning was strong on faith.

The walk from the church to the Yankee camp was short. Such was the commotion that I could not find the corporal again. Six steamboats were at the landing loading men and provisions. As many more were on the far bank or mid-stream. A great effort was being made to cross the Yankee camp over to the fortress that was indeed surrendering.

Anatilda had a red dress and matching berege talma that she often wore to town or church. She did not let the season interfere with her fondness for this eye-catching suit. I saw the flash of the dress as she gestured to Mink from the middle deck of a boat taking on hogsheads of flour. She looked toward me, and I stepped quickly behind a wagon. The movement came without conscious thought as a rider who grabs for a dislodged cap. I did not budge while black men rolled barrels down the gangway and stood them on end where a soldier pointed. In time the walk was lifted, the bell rang, and the boat backed away for the crossing. Anger came over me then—not anger at Anatilda but at myself for letting her presence make me feel ashamed.

Not until the early afternoon did I manage to cross on a small steamer that served as a courier for Admiral Porter. Her kind captain yielded to my perjury with sympathy drawn from personal loss. He said that like me he hoped to rescue an injured brother but that his chances of getting to a place called Belle Isle were dim.

At that time I had never been to a town as big as Vicksburg. In an ordinary situation it would have seemed fascinating to me. How can I even begin to tell of the feel of this day?

The landing was bustling. Men and mules labored to haul freight up the long cut in the bluff to the city. I heard that it was mostly food for the Rebel soldiers who had been living on a biscuit a day. Dust of a peculiar type, finer than flour, lay shoe-mouth deep in the roads. It billowed like a heavy cloud with the least disturbance and was terrible in the heat. A new and splendid courthouse was the pride of the town. It stood upon the highest point and challenged gunboat sailors upstream and down. This great building became my target also as I knew of no better place to begin my search for Minor.

The streets above the landing were full of people, mostly Yankee soldiers going to and fro purposefully. Town people were standing on the plank sidewalks and sitting on front porches watching—watching to see where this turn of events would take them. If they were relieved that shells were no longer falling on their houses, it did not show on the faces of these women, children and old men. It was not possible to read the faces of young southern men because there were none in sight.

I was surprised that the buildings had not been leveled to the ground during the many days and nights of bombardment. A person ignorant of the circumstances and dropped into certain places of the town might for a while not even notice the evidence. During the siege repairs had been made quickly with whatever materials were available. A closer look would reveal fresh patches on the roofs, a porch post that did not match, and window panes broken to the very last one.

The courthouse was different. It was like the southern army now, ragged and beaten, robbed of hope and glory, with future unknown. My own hopes diminished as I stood looking up at the pocked sentinel.

To get a lay of the town I climbed the courthouse hill, weaving among craters, and sat in the shade of the building. The Old Glory flag was freshly raised atop the courthouse. It hung limp at an odd angle from a hoe-handle pole. When I looked at it, the song "Victory In Jesus" came into my mind. It was a crazy thought, but I could not shake the melody.

Hell probably looks like the hills east of the courthouse did on that afternoon. They were naked and yellow. Only a few trees with broken, scarecrow limbs were left. Green was not a color to be seen, and gray-clad men milled about on one distant ridge.

I did not see anyone close by who looked as though he might help me. Many large houses were north of the courthouse. I decided to walk south though, back toward the business establishments. When an old woman rounded a corner and was about to pass me by, I asked, "Mam, can you tell me where I might find the soldiers' hospital?" These words, the first that I had spoken in the state of Mississippi, came out distressed and too fast. The old woman stopped and stared at me with heavy eyes. There was patience in her answer.

"Child, this town is full of hospitals and all of 'em are soldiers' hospitals. Them that ain't in private homes are being nursed by the Sisters of Charity. Theirs are marked by yeller hospital flags. Go down here to Clay Street just at the corner." She reached and grasped my arm for a moment before walking away.

The yellow flag hung from a sign on a three-floored building. Before the battle it was a books and stationary store—Brooks, Burnell and Company. A Yankee soldier boy stood on duty outside the open door and nodded politely to me as I went in. For a moment I could not see. When my eyes fixed to the darkness, I saw a row of beds down each brick wall leading into the shadows. The beds closest to the door were empty. The air was stifling and foul. A strong feeling came over me to run from this place. Only a real voice stopped me.

"May I help you?" A nun in brown habit came forward from the dimness. She was plump and spoke with an accent that I thought was French.

"I am looking for my brother who was wounded." I have since decided that I cannot lie without sounding foolish. The nun stared at me.

Finally she asked, "Does your brother have a name and home?"

"Minor Barrett from Union Parish, Louisiana."

"He is not here and has not been here," she said as a matter of fact.

"Are you sure?"

"Quite. Only boys from Mississippi and a few from Alabama are sent here. It's a rule from the queer owner of the building. Go to the warehouse. It is our largest hospital. You must hurry because tonight the Yankees will begin loading many of the patients aboard boats to New Orleans where medicine and doctors are plentiful."

The warehouse was part way down the river bluff. It seemed a strange place for a hospital because it was exposed to the gunboats. Sister Chloe was in charge. She said the Yankees knew the purpose of this building and dropped their bombs beyond it in the town and trenches. She assured me that God's will saw to this matter except that for some strange reason He did let one shell fall into their well and ruin it just last week to their great dismay. "Besides," she said, "there is death enough here as it is."

I knew Sister Chloe was French because she called me "cher" like Mrs. Barrett did. Her voice was pleasant in a peaceful way and calmed me as I am sure it did her patients. I thought she would have been a good grandmother.

"More than a hundred men lie here today," she said. "Most suffer from debilitas, not injury. If your brother be amongst them he'll be at the back with the wounded."

"His name is Minor Barrett from Louisiana," I told her.

"I do not remember names in this place. They lay on my soul."

Still, she checked the dead list back to May and did not find Minor's name.

This hospital was dark too. Most light came in one of the open wagon doors and through slits in warped battens on the walls. It was cooler this way, and besides, flies shy away from shadows.

Sister Chloe told me to go down the center aisle and begin my search just beyond a half bale of cotton that was used to dress wounds. I do not remember the walk, but I know that I did not look to the side for fear of what I might see.

At the bale I stopped and forced myself to look. Fifteen or twenty cots lined the walls from this point on to more wagon doors at the end of the warehouse. In these beds were my greatest hopes and darkest fears. I tried to look at them all at once without focusing. They held lumps, some of them not whole people lumps. The lumps jerked and coughed, or they were still. From a few beds eyes bored into me, but not those dark eyes that had stared into mine and exposed my heart on Bayou de l'Outre. These were desperate eyes and despairing eyes. I think they were eyes yearning mostly for the sight of their mothers.

Nothing is blacker than a crow's wing and nothing shines brighter in a sunbeam—nothing but Minor's hair. The light flowed through a crack in the wall and spilled onto the back of Minor's head. Though he faced away from me, I recognized him at once.

"He sleeps much of the time." Sister Chloe was standing behind me. Maybe I had been staring at him for a long time.

"I have come to take him home," I said.

"It is best not to wake him now. I cannot release him until he signs the parole papers, and that will be tomorrow. Let him save his rest, cher."

Sister Chloe left to tend a calling soldier. I knelt down beside Minor's cot and studied him. His face was new to me because I had never seen him unshaven. His short black beard looked soft and I wanted to touch it, but I did not just yet. He wore a shirt that I recognized as one given to him by Mrs. Carter when he returned from school. Some short person's gray wool trousers came half way up to his knees. He was barefoot, though his tall boots stood at the foot of the bed. I could not see an injury. There were no apparent ragged scars or pools of blood as I had beheld in my nightmares. He was pale, but he did not seem near death. To me he was beautiful.

I watched him until suddenly I became afraid—afraid that he would wake up and see me—and because I did not have words ready to speak, ready to tell him why I was at his bedside at this moment. There was nothing to do but hurry away in a near panic, but not before I leaned over and kissed his brow.

Sister Chloe stopped me at the front door and told me of Minor's condition. Her records showed that he had been brought here on May 18th, after the battle at the Big Black River. She said that he had been shot in the hip, with the ball passing clean through and exiting near his groin. For a month they had thought he would die, but the gangrene did not come and he lived. He had begun walking only a few days before, and too many steps started the bleeding again. Sister Chloe told me to come back the next morning at 10 o'clock with transportation for him. As I left my finally found darling, the sun was setting fast over the Louisiana swamps.

Chapter 10

I soon discovered that the hotels were all full of Yankees. A stingy woman offered me a bed in a cave for more gold than it was worth, and I took it. Many people had lived in caves dug from the yellow clay hills during the siege. They were bomb-proof and fixed up nicely. A merchant's wife who had moved with her children back into their proper house earlier in the day owned the cave where I stayed. Rugs covered the walls and floor, and a sheet was pinned to the ceiling. No earth was exposed, but I still felt like I was under the ground. A wash stand with a china basin and pitcher provided some relief. A tallow candle lit my supper of jerked beef and a pear. When I climbed into the rusty bed, I did not think of the menacing worry that should have been on my mind. Instead I argued with myself about whether my lips had actually touched Minor's skin.

Fleas bit me in the night, and I woke itching and scratching in the morning. Fatigue and the darkness of the cave had caused me to sleep later than I had planned. Already soldiers were marching on the street to the tapping cadence of a Yankee drummer boy. This northern army looked disciplined and well under control of its officers. I even saw a Yankee soldier under guard on Washington Street, standing on a barrel with a "thief" sign around his neck. I did not see them boiling babies for breakfast as some southerners claimed.

My first task of the day was to find a horse or mule with a buggy to carry Minor down to the landing. It did not take me long to figure out that stock could not be hired at any price in this town. The starving Confederate soldiers had eaten it all. Only a few milking cows survived, and they were guarded and cherished along with the black wet nurses to keep the babies of Vicksburg alive. Of course there were plenty of horses and mules belonging to the Yankee army, but they were hard at work doing the business of General Grant. I was scared to ask for their help for fear that it might draw unnecessary attention to Minor. I wanted to slip him away without fuss or commotion.

A street ran along the bluffs. Here southern batteries had guarded the fortress and broken the back of the river to Yankee navigation for many months. I figure Admiral Porter had cursed these guns regularly unless he was a religious man. They fired the iron of the city into his fleet at every chance. Now companies of Yankee artillerymen swarmed over the batteries and prepared to carry the cannons away. I walked south through this tumult and began to feel desperate again for a plan.

Those prayers of mine that are short and simple are the ones God answers most often. I think it is because He does not have time to listen to the long, drawn-out pleadings of so many people. Besides, He already knows the story and just wants us to ask for his blessings instead of being proud. The answer to my first prayer of this day was leaning on end against a walnut stump beside the road. It was a fine wheelbarrow, the kind without sides used to haul bricks. No one was around to claim it, so I borrowed it without permission or guilt.

By this time it was approaching mid-morning and I was more than two miles from the hospital. The axle on the wheelbarrow was worn, making its hurried path look like the trail of a frantic snake in the dust. Weaving through the traffic I reached the warehouse just as the church bells struck ten o'clock.

Sister Chloe was sweeping at the front doors when I arrived. She looked up and seemed a bit surprised to see me.

"Well cher, who do you come after now?" she asked.

"I come for Minor—my brother—as you told me yesterday. It is ten o'clock."

She looked at me curiously. "Yes, it is ten o'clock for sure, but your sister-in-law left with her husband an hour ago."

The shock of these words drove me back a step. "No!" was all that I could cry.

"When I asked of you, she acted angry. She said you were lazy and waiting for them at the boat. Did you confuse the arrangement?"

I ran past her through the hospital to Minor's bed. It was empty just as she had said.

Sister Chloe caught up with me. "What is the matter, cher? Something is not right." She was becoming as distressed as me. "They put him on an army horse. I told them he could not ride that way, but she did not listen. She would not even take his belongings and threw this against the wall when she saw it." Sister Chloe reached down and picked up a flour sack in the corner. She handed it to me slowly as though afraid that I might hurl it at her too. I opened it to behold the painting of me from Bayou de l'Outre.

I cannot describe the state of my emotions in these moments. My senses blurred to freeze me in place, totally incapable of thought or action. My vision was reduced to a tunnel of smudged shadows directly in front of my eyes. I did not feel the heat, smell the lingering death in this place, nor taste my own tears. Only my ears were acute to the world. From the edge of the tunnel they heard these words crisp and clear:

"Whom do you seek?"

"Minor Barrett," I whispered desperately.

"I am Minor Barrett," came the reply.

Then from the other side of the tunnel, "Minor Barrett—that will be me. I will go with you."

I whirled around to face this new assertion only to hear another behind me claim, "No, Minor Barrett is my name. Take me with you." A fourth man near the front door made the same appeal through wheezing coughs. For the second time I ran from this place.

An empty livery stable backed up to the bluff just down the street from the hospital. Below it a single mimosa tree held tight on the steep slope. Here I used Mr. Carter's hunting knife to cut off my hair. The locks whose touch once made Minor quiver with anticipation piled into my lap and spilled into the dust. I sat under the tree for most of the day and watched hummingbirds fly to and from the tree's pink flowers. My thoughts raced away and returned with the birds all afternoon, but they alone found nourishment.

When the heat of the day had passed, for no good reason I climbed back up to the road and walked by the Prentiss House Hotel down toward the river. The hurry was gone from the landing. So too were some of the warships, though a long row of boats still nosed up to the mud bank with gangplanks stuck out like so many skinny tongues. Willow trees leaning toward the water shaded scattered knots of Confederate soldiers. Tension that for months nearly sucked away the breath of Vicksburg had moved on to another waiting battlefield. The town was no longer in-between.

I stopped and inquired of one group of the paroled soldiers. They were from Claiborne Parish. Their captain, who still wore his gilded sword, said no boats were allowed to cross the river today because of rumors that regiments of Texas cavalry had arrived on the far shore. Some transports loaded with wounded and sick had left for New Orleans, and others were leaving in the morning. The captain said we had little chance of crossing until the next evening. Then, to the soldiers I must have appeared dumbstruck, for less than a stag's leap away walked Mink, green-eyed and hair the color of oak flowers, leading a bob-tailed horse up the cut. He did not see me, for I used the soldiers as a screen until he went out of sight over the hill. I followed him at once.

Mink went straight to a big red-brick house that served as a headquarters for the Yankees. I slipped along the wall of the house next door until I could conceal myself under a thick rose arbor. Mink tied the horse to the picket fence, climbed the steps, and spoke to a guard at the front door. The guard went in and soon returned, followed by a fat, hog-jowled Yankee officer with a cordial in his hand. This man walked around the horse looking her over carefully. Finally, he turned toward Mink and spoke in a high squeaky voice, "Tell your fancy mistress she kin rent my horse anytime. The price'll be the same." He hitched up his pants and whistled a jig back into the house. I did not know what to make of the situation then, but I do now.

Mink left the house and backtracked. He walked back through town and down the cut to the landing. He went downstream on the sandbar past the boats and the groups of soldiers. I stayed far enough behind to avoid being detected. The sun was beginning to set and fired the looming bluffs on our left with the flat streams of evening light. Tall, limber willows grew nearest the foot of the bluffs, and others became ever shorter as they marched across the newer sands toward the river. Mink plodded on for a half mile and finally turned into the thicket out of my sight. I continued on beyond for a short way, crossed a small stream that ran into the river, and also turned in toward the bluff, never crossing his tracks. He had stopped.

Darkness came on, and I soon heard the noise of their camp. Mink was beating driftwood limbs against a tree to break them into firewood. A panther never stalked his prey quieter than I crept forward. The sand swallowed my footfall, and sparks rising from their fire and dying in the river breeze led me in. The camp lay where springs and seeps at the foot of the bluff joined to make the stream, which in a few hundred feet flowed into the river. Anatilda sat under a mosquito bar and watched Mink cook supper on the too-hot fire. I could not see Minor, but a lean-to stood in the shadows and I figured he was there. An hour passed while they cooked and ate and laid their bedding. During this time Mink carried food to the lean-to. Soon they settled for the night, and I began to think of my plight. This situation was so different from any that I had imagined. I could not recollect ideas that would guide me forward from the mind-full of plans in my head. So I just squatted there in the mosquitoes, brooding, but not for long.

Anatilda sat up and called out, "Mink ----- Mink!"

"I'z heah, Miz Tilda." He sounded weary. "Don't be skeered."

"Git up, you fool, and light the candles. I'm gonna look at him."

Mink rose and rustled around in a pack. He found a candle and lit it in the fire.

"Miz Tilda, you bes let him res. He been wore out today."

Anatilda was up now. She ordered him, "Bring the light."

They went to the lean-to, and as they moved so did I, around and much closer. The fire was now behind the lean-to and forged crisp shadows on the thin canvas wall. Anatilda and Mink stood over Minor as he lay on a low cot.

She spoke to him sweetly, "Minor darling, I am going to examine your injury. You are my husband, remember. We were married and you left before I could enjoy the pleasures of being your wife."

Minor stirred but did not speak.

"Pull down his pants," she told Mink.

Mink did this and I heard Minor groan. I became aware then that my fingers hurt from squeezing the handle of Mr. Carter's large hunting knife. I do not know how long I had clutched it to my breast; it happened without thoughts.

"Move the bandages aside and give me the candle," Anatilda urged her slave. On the canvas her silhouette was traced into the shape of a preying mantis. She looked closely at Minor and stepped back quickly. After a moment she passed judgment: "He's ruined." Anatilda said this in a final way like a guilty verdict, and the feelings in her voice suddenly relieved me of worries long pushed into the back corners of my mind. Hope sprang forth once again.

Anatilda left the lean-to and walked to the edge of the firelight. She stared into the darkness for a while and then called to Mink again, "Fetch the boat. We'll cross tonight."

Mink began to beg.

"Miz Tilda, we drown fer sho. Dis ain't de Bayou l'Outre. Dis de mighty Mississip. I cain't swim a lick and dem suckholes'll take us straight down to hell. Please les wait on de light."

He carried on so and it was pitiful to hear him, but Anatilda would have none of it. Finally he got quiet and accepted his fate for the duration of the crime. He waded off down the stream and soon came back pulling a small bateau. They got Minor up, and Mink practically carried him to the boat. Anatilda climbed into the back and sat on the only seat, holding a candle. I watched this tiny light fade away as Mink pulled them back down the shallow creek toward the river. When I walked through the camp to follow, it did not strike me as peculiar that they had left all their belongings behind.

The stream cut through a long, wide sandbar to enter the river. The moon was not full, but, in the open away from the trees, forms were obvious and the currents danced with quicksilver. Up the river, watch lights showed from atop the row of boats at the landing, and the breeze bore lonesome notes of fiddle music down from the bluff. Only the squawk of a night heron saved me from detection by Anatilda and Mink. I had pursued them closer than I had thought, and when the bateaux startled the bird I was close enough to hear them clearly again. They were at the mouth of the stream.

"Gittin' deep up heah, Miz Tilda."

"Hie on Mink. Your knees are dry yet." She talked as if in a trance.

"I feels de quicksan' on my laig. I bes git in now."

The next thing I hear is a loud splash and Anatilda cussin' Mink like the devil himself. I ran closer and saw Anatilda waist deep behind the boat pushing it out into the river with all her might. Mink was standing aside. With one final shove she cried out, "Be gone!" and turned back toward the shore. Just as the pharaoh did to boy babies in the time of Moses, Anatilda cast poor Minor into the river. Current grabbed the bateaux, spun it crossways for a better grip, and hauled it onward.

Mink's words reflected my thoughts too. "You done finish what de Yankees started, Miz Tilda. He a daid man now." Anatilda waded back up the stream with Mink in tow.

When I was a small child in my mother's village, two nightmares often came late in the night, finding me deep in the folds of trade blankets. One carried a fire demon that appeared suddenly and always consumed my mother's shoes before cornering me. Every time, I yielded without a struggle and was devoured by the fire. I had no shoes in those days.

The other nightmare began as I was sent to fetch water from a well on a dark, cloudy day. The well had a low curbing, and I always fell in. I always knew I would fall in. A hand deep in the cold water would grab my foot and try to pull me down. In this dream I never gave up. I kicked until I woke crying and upset my mother.

After the night on the river below Vicksburg, this nightmare began to visit me again and still does from time to time.

Chapter 11

I never let the bateaux out of my sight. It slid along the surface of the river almost faster than I could walk along the sandbar. Fifty yards offshore it jerked and spun violently in a whirlpool before settling down again. The current was running close to the bank in this outside bend, but I could see that it would soon cross to the middle as the river turned. Shadowy trees up ahead marked the end of the sandbar where the bluffs once again advanced right up to the deep water.

I cannot say that I weighed the risks to my life before I ran into the river and began to swim toward the boat. I suppose there was no time for such considerations. The response was not different from lunging desperately to catch a crystal salt-cellar that has been bumped over the edge of the kitchen table.

The current was stronger than I had reckoned. I was able to wade halfway to the boat before being forced to swim, and even then it was ahead of me. I knew I could never catch up. I struggled back to the bank and ran ahead to take a better course that would allow me to capture the vessel as it came by. In doing so I lost sight of the boat and for a time thought it had sunk. When it reappeared, it bore straight down on me and I had no trouble grasping the bow.

An instant later I tasted the bile of terror caused by foolishness. It came up suddenly in my throat and lingered during the long crisis of the moment. Without thinking I tried to heave myself into the front of the boat. My effort was not balanced, and the boat tipped. Minor cried out and rolled to the low side. Water rushed in. The bateaux rose and began to slide sideways under the surface like a saucer in a dishpan. Only when I turned loose and pushed away did the boat settle. The damage was done. A third full of water, it floundered and raced with the current for the middle of the river. Drained of purpose and plan I held tight to the stern and was towed into my nightmare.

The Mississippi River is as alive as any great creature made by God. Muscles of currents push and pull the brown waters into tender caresses and terrifying wrenches. It consumes—giant cottonwoods and steamboats, plantations and towns, the plans of generals and foolish girls. If not burdened with a soul, then surely it possesses a will.

I managed to get the small pack that still hung over my shoulder into the bateaux and discovered that Mr. Carter's knife had slipped from my belt during the frenzy. The river began to toy with me then, flowing smooth and silky around my body, promising and almost warm. Just as my mind began to clear and rational thoughts to appear, a long sipping sound, like one makes when in a hurry to drink hot coffee, came from the darkness into which the boat was drifting. The sipping became the tearing of a mile-long bed sheet as we raced into whirlpools and riptides of ice water. From one moment to the next the boiling currents would seem almost to push me up out of the river, prod me brutishly, and then jerk me violently toward a bottom that defined terror. In these times I was forced to think of the beasts of the black depths, especially when something brushed against my bare legs or thumped against the boat. I had once seen a garfish longer than a wagon bed that had been shot as he lay trapped in a drying pool of Bayou D'Arbonne in the summertime. If the D'Arbonne could harbor such a brute, what of the mighty Mississippi? Bigger ones for sure, and giant eels and loggerheads, and sharks up from the ocean, and what about the descendents of Jonah's fish? Throughout the night I dangled there like bait for them all until a verse of Mrs. Barrett's favorite poetry finally came to comfort me from the romance of Atala:

> *Great God, from your just furor*
> *Spare the poor voyager!*

Minor was quiet and stirred only during the few times I cried out in spite of myself. As the stars faded into the early morning light, I was able to see my lover clearly for the first time since the hospital. He lay on his back in the boat, head toward the bow and legs almost floating in water from the near tip-over. He wore the same clothes and had his tall boots on. The water had soothed his fevers, and he breathed peacefully with his eyes closed.

During the night we had drifted a long ways and were now close to the west bank of the river. I could not see any other vessels, but smoke from those at the Vicksburg landing climbed the sky to the north. Suddenly my feet touched bottom. This surprised me greatly because we were still a quarter mile from the shore. A large sandbar rose up and the water was soon no more than knee deep. I was able to push the boat toward the shore and made good progress until another deep channel cut away the bottom. Encouraged, I pointed the bow across the current and kicked. After a while we drifted up against a small sawyer, spun around, and the river shallowed again, this time for good.

When the bateaux nudged the bank, I looked at Minor and he was staring at me intently. "Do you know me?" I asked.

He reached out with two fingers and touched the small scar on my side. "Yes, oh yes," was his reply, and bewilderment was in his expression.

When he struggled to sit up, I helped him. Then I noticed he was wasted from his ordeal. The working flesh was gone from his bones. He felt frail in my arms, and delicate.

"Do not strain yourself. We will talk later. First we must seek shade before the sun is higher."

With his arm over my shoulders Minor could walk well enough once we got started. I aimed for a tall planertree whose crown jutted above the others on the second bank, and after an hour with many rests we reached the tree. I emptied the possibles pack onto the ground and found nothing fit to eat and most of the few medicines ruined. A weakness came over me then, and I could not rise from my knees. The river had drained me of strength, and though it was not my conscious bidding, I lay down and slept.

It was after noon when I woke, very hungry. Minor was lying on his side sleeping in the deep, dry leaves. Green flies swarmed about his blood-stained britches. I knew that he needed food even more than I, so I began to forage along the bank. Possum grapes were plentiful. They were mealy but quenched the thirst, and I filled the pack. On the way back to the big planertree I decided to go immediately for Chula in order to transport Minor. It did not occur to me then that I had no idea where to carry him. He was still asleep when I returned with the grapes and seemed groggy when I told him I was going for help. He just nodded in a dazed manner when I insisted that he eat.

I did not know it then, but we were on the edge of White's Plantation, which straddles the throat of land that leads to DeSoto Point. I had crossed this place a mile to the north only days before and was at this time no more than five miles from Chula. I walked north and soon came to a road alongside a cotton field. The railroad ran through the field in the distance. I stayed on the road until it crossed the railroad and followed the tracks east. With the sun at my back I hurried on to Atlas' hut beneath the trestle.

I knew that Minor could not travel far in his condition and wondered if he could even manage to ride Chula at all. He certainly could not survive the journey back to Iron Branch, a place that now felt more dangerous to me than the wounds of a hundred Yankee bullets. The idea that I had saved Minor from a demon only to share in her guilt stuck in my mind. I wished for the counsel of my mother, whom I remembered as being wise in troubled times.

Atlas was sitting on the burned-out trestle over his hut watching me come down the tracks. He stood up as I approached, his toothless gums shining in a grin. With his staff he poked at three adjacent crossties and then poked at others, skipping one in between. He swung his arms in an exaggerated manner. It took me a few moments to figure out that he was mocking me. The ties did not fit my gait. They were too close together to step on each one, and stepping over one stretched my pace. Atlas cheered my spirit then and in days to come.

Chula squealed and brayed like a colt in a yellow jacket nest when first he smelled me. Quint led me down a dim trail behind the hut to a small corral made by nailing single rails between trees in a palmetto thicket. An old, caved-in brick cistern held water that the boy drawed with a rope and lard tin to pour in a half-log trough. If anything, the little mule had gained weight, for he was surrounded by his favorite treat—poison vines. He had nibbled them as high as he could reach over much of the pen. I was glad to see that he was well cared for but apprehensive that his racket would bring unwanted attention to our situation. Only when I allowed him to walk behind me with his nose in the small of my back did he settle down.

Back at Atlas' hut I retrieved the undisturbed belongings I had left there before crossing to Vicksburg and loaded them onto Chula. When I tried to pay Atlas another gold piece, he would not take it. Instead he tied Chula's lead rope to a piling, took me by the hand, and led me to sit on a rough bench against his hut. He summoned the boy for an interpreter and began to make throat noises and gestures that only Quint could understand.

"Atlas say, where's yo man?" said the boy.

I had not told Atlas directly about Minor but in these things of the heart he had special knowledge.

"He is on the downstream river bank near White's Plantation. He is badly wounded." I said.

Atlas pointed to the sky and then me.

"Atlas say, 'Where you goin'?'" said the boy.

This question I could not answer and my despair poured forth again. This time I had an audience—one that saved my life. Atlas hushed my sobbing and made me sit up straight against the hut while I told my story and Minor's. Down on one knee and leaning on his staff, he urged me on until it was all out and I was left hollow. He walked away then, blacker than wet coal and taller than the trees.

He came back in a few minutes and called the boy. Their conversation was hard, and Quint could not understand all of the old man's gibberish. Finally, Atlas went into the hut and returned with a fine, blue china saucer. The boy caught on immediately and the plans were made.

"Atlas say, 'Don't you worry none missus,'" said the boy. "He say we'z goin' to where Sudie live. Meet you and the soljer man on de White's place road in der mornin'."

Trusting Atlas came natural for me. Without asking a single question about Sudie or where she lived, I left with Chula and some potatoes from the small garden beside the hut and a jug of sweet water. That a good man could have his tongue cut out by professed saviors captured my thoughts during the walk back to Minor.

He was sitting up taking inventory of his possessions when I returned at dusk. Other than the clothes on his back they consisted of a small, bone-handled jack-knife and a broken nit comb. We ate the potatoes and slept under the big planertree, not knowing what the morrow would bring.

Soon after first light I convinced Chula to stand still beside a log so that Minor could mount. When we reached the road Atlas and Quint were squatting in the dust where my tracks from the day before had entered the forest. They had brought a companion. Quint called him Uncle Jeff but was quick to explain that he was no kin to Jeff Davis. He said he was probably older than Jeff Davis anyway. Uncle Jeff was surely the oldest billy goat that I had ever seen, and he had the horns to prove it. One pointed sideways and one pointed forward, just like his eyeballs. He wore a braided grapevine collar with a red leather harness and was dragging a travois that held a wrapped bundle. Chula did not like him then or ever.

Without saying much we walked west down the road in a single line. Atlas marched in front followed by Quint leading the goat. I led Chula and Minor several steps to the rear. During this journey Chula never let Uncle Jeff get behind him. Most of the time he kept him pointed with stiff ears like a bird dog. Chula knew something of trust also.

After a while the road crossed another of General Grant's canals. It was nearly dry, with planks laid across its bed. No one was around, and we passed over without trouble. Houses were scarce, and we kept up a good pace until mid-morning when Atlas signaled for a rest.

Before we started again this man, whom I was now convinced had once been a mighty African king, inspected his entourage. Quint got a pat on the head and Uncle Jeff's collar was adjusted. He held my hand briefly in a gesture of steadiness. Chula's feet were examined, and to my amazement he stood quietly while Atlas carved a shallow V in his hoof to stop a running split. Minor got the most attention though. Atlas looked deeply into his eyes while pushing up and pulling down Minor's eyelids with his thumbs. Atlas frowned but made no effort to share his diagnosis. Instead he helped Minor mount Chula and we continued on. The pace was faster now.

Our path left the railroad at Walnut Bayou and followed the stream southwest, then west. A steam mill and plantations lined the banks of this shallow, narrow bayou. The land was good, but the crops were ill kept and many fields were fallow. Most of the people we saw were black and avoided us. Yankees had occupied this country for many months.

At Dr. Dancy's place we left the road and took a trail through the woods to cut off a big bend in the bayou as it turned north. In the late afternoon we came upon the bayou again and crossed in front of a Mrs. Hamilton's house. She gave us well water when I asked and stared more than a little at our parade.

We soon left all signs of civilization behind and entered a great unbroken woods. Atlas led us through a pathless cathedral of giant trees that swallowed all but the deep shadows of sunlight. Vines with the girth of my leg snaked up huge red gums and striped oaks. So large were these titans that in their death throes an acre was flattened. Other forests grew under the big trees. Palmetto fans crowded the flats and shoved their way to the edge of ridges where dense armies of cane held them at bay. The cane talked too—in dry, murmuring threats to invaders and whispers of hope for knowing sojourners. I think God visits this place more often than others I have seen.

My worries about Minor being able to ride came true. He did not complain although his face revealed the growing pain of his wounds. Without a road the going was hard with many downed trees and thickets to avoid. The little blind mule high-stepped as best he could but still stumbled on occasion and jolted Minor in a terrible way. When a kunti vine nearly brought them both to the ground I called for Atlas to stop.

He inspected Minor's eyes again and rubbed Chula's forelegs. He made the boy understand that our destination was not much farther. Quint passed along this message, and we walked straight into the setting sun leaving the long summer day behind.

Before the whole of night fell upon us we came to the Tensas River and the road that ran along its high bank. Turning south, we walked for two more hours in the darkness before finally arriving at the place where Sudie lived.

Atlas's half-sister was well fixed. She lived in a large two-room cabin of squared gum logs. A dogtrot separated the rooms and joined porches front and back. Chimneys of river-clay bricks rose at each end to draft the cooking and heating fires and masked this place as a home of slaves. Sudie built her story over the coming weeks one layer at a time, like a swallow constructs her nest of mud.

She had been born and reared on a plantation in north Mississippi. When her owner died after fifteen years, she was auctioned on the block in Memphis and bought by Mr. Weingard. He was a peculiar man with peculiar ideas about slavery. He owned a strip of virgin land along the Tensas River and brought his plans and fifty slaves to this place. Only by a quirk of fate did she come to live within a few miles of her much older half-brother, Atlas, whom she barely remembered and rediscovered through rumors.

Her new master went about his business by pairing up the single men and women into couples, clearing the good land along the river, and planting the first crops. After five years the place began to operate like a normal plantation. Then Mr. Weingard gathered the slaves and revealed his designs. He spoke of his love for all races of men and his general dislike of bondage. He told them that his ancestors, like them, were once slaves. For this reason he proposed to give them some freedoms in return for loyalty and work on his land. They must still work together for the common goal of making the plantation profitable—he said this was the most important thing. But they could build good cabins and they could choose their own sites away from the crowded quarters if they wished. He told them they could elect two leaders from among their own ranks to serve as work bosses. He promised no more white overseers if all went well. Problems, he said, would not be addressed by whippings but by a quick sale down the river. He told them also that he planned to move to Natchez and visit often.

Later, one other innocent proposal was revealed before he left. It shook the plantation like a second mighty earthquake. Mr. Weingard knew of troubles between some couples and admitted mistakes in his matchmaking. He offered to undo marriages and allow them to choose their own mates if all involved agreed. Imagine the turmoil. Sudie said the place flamed hotter than grease fires for weeks over the matter until Mr. Weingard put a stop to the squabbling. In the end, seven couples were remarried on Easter Sunday and encouraged to peacefully fill the plantation with children. Those who had quarreled the most were not among them for want of a suitable swap.

Sudie got a new man then. Jasper, her first husband, had openly declared his fondness for the fat and widowed cook, Cindy. Sudie gladly let him go and soon began to receive suitors of her own. She chose handsome Beck to live with her and a five-year old daughter. At eighteen, Beck was two years younger than Sudie and unmarried. He was trained as a mechanic and worked in the gin and blacksmith shop. Sudie knew that only the smartest Negroes got these jobs.

Early on, Beck proved to be a good husband. They picked a cabin site on the far end of Rainey Lake, a quarter mile from the others, and built the first room, working mostly on Sundays and at night. In a year Sudie had twin boys, but they came early and were buried close to the back door to keep wolves from digging up the graves. Afterwards Sudie could bear no more children. Beck's calm, steady nature and skill as a broker eventually led to his election as boss of the craft workers, everyone but the field hands. The couple added a room to the cabin and lived well until the war came.

Mr. Weingard's enterprise flourished for a while. The rich flush of the new-ground yielded generous crops for a few years and cotton prices were high. Knowing no other way of life, the slaves continued their work as before and enjoyed the new liberties. Problems arose, but maybe no more than normal, and Mr. Weingard kept his word. One man was sold for poisoning a mule, two others for general laziness after many warnings.

The Tensas plantation was isolated. Small steamboats could come for the cotton only on the very high waters of late winter. Some years it had to be hauled out by wagon, the way Mr. Weingard brought in most of the supplies. Visitors were usually those few who passed on the river road to and from the other remote plantations in the swamp. For this reason rumors of war were much slower in reaching the people than those who lived just fifteen miles to the east on the Mississippi River plantations. When the rumors did come, the place changed.

Mr. Weingard's body servant was the source of the early news. He rode to the plantation from Natchez with his master on each visit. His eager audience heard first the whispered gossip and later the bold facts. Every trip roused emotions of hope, fear, anger, and joy. Firmer words of real freedom finally gelled into a changed attitude for most of the slaves.

Sudie said that Beck was transformed. To her he was talking crazy. He said he wanted to run away and work for himself fixing other people's gins and get paid with real money. He said he wanted to buy a black top hat for himself and a yellow ruffled dress for Sudie to wear at the New Year's dance. When word came that the Yankees were at Lake Providence and welcoming slaves to join them for work on the canals, Beck left with many others.

With no white overseers and Mr. Weingard's now-scarce visits, there was nothing or nobody to stop them.

When we arrived at Sudie's house, Beck had been gone a year and she had heard from him once. A slave from the next plantation south had come back, escaped he said, bringing a message that begged her to stay at home and saying that he had run away to Hell. I thought of the fresh graves in the levee when she told me this story.

Chapter 12

When we walked into Sudie's yard on the night of July 7, 1863, I did not expect to stay for four months. Her cur dogs raised such a fuss that Uncle Jeff nearly broke his neck spinning around trying to keep them all in view at once. As it was, he upset the travois.

The ruckus brought Sudie to the door hollerin', "Who deah? Who out deah?"

Atlas and the boy went forward onto the porch. The boy spoke in an excited manner to the shadow behind the cracked door.

"It yo brother Atlas, an' his frien' Quint, and Miz Bita the white woman, and her soljer man what's shot in two."

No doubt we nearly scared poor Sudie to death. Strange visitors in the night did not bode well in those times. Directly, a candle was lit and thrust out through the crack. Satisfied, she opened the door and scolded the still-yapping dogs. Atlas and the boy followed her into the cabin.

After what seemed like a long while they came out, Sudie giving orders to every black person in sight. She told Atlas to help Minor inside. A slender girl who seemed to appear from the vapors was directed to lead Chula to a three-rail lot beside the cabin and provide him with fodder. She charged Quint with the task of convincing Uncle Jeff that it was in his best interest to spend the night in an empty corncrib. Goodness was in her voice, and I liked her from the start.

One room of the cabin was a kitchen and parlor. The other held two handmade beds for Sudie and the girl, who was her daughter, and a tiny baby. Minor was laid on Sudie's bed and I was shown the other. When I politely but steadfastly refused to take the bed of the young mother and her baby, Sudie helped me get settled on a nest of straw and rags in the low loft over the parlor. She tucked me in and left with encouraging words. "We'll do better tomorrow. Eat then too." I was too tired for cares or hunger and quickly fell into my dreams.

The next day began to reveal our new home and the character of our hosts. The smell of boiling corn-meal coffee woke me. Sudie was up early frying chickens that she had snatched from the roost. When the chicken was done she spooned meal mixed with hot water into the grease. For some reason, perhaps the intensity of the circumstances, this breakfast sticks in my mind as the best I have eaten before or since.

With one exception the house contained the barest of domestic necessities. Other than the rope beds, crude benches and a rough table were the only furniture. Cooking ware consisted of an iron pot and gourds of various sizes. Scanty personal items were stored in split oak baskets against the wall.

The single hint of means was stacked on a kitchen shelf – four plates and three saucers of blue china – identical to the piece in Atlas' hut. The pattern was of a coach carrying fine ladies and driven by a man in a top hat. A story hid behind these treasures, an intrigue, but I was never able to find it in spite of subtle inquiry.

Sudie made arrangements for our extended stay. Quint and the girl, whose name was Mirah, were sent to gather moss that draped the surrounding trees. Wonderful bedding was produced when the moss was stuffed into cotton sacks sewn shut with a cobbler's needle. Each night Sudie laid her mattress in a corner of the parlor while Atlas and Quint bedded down in the dogtrot. I spread mine in the loft and never yearned for more comfort.

I could see Atlas in Sudie's bones. She was tall and moved with natural grace. The skin of her face was flawless and pulled tight over sharp cheekbones. Her hair was cropped close into tiny black curls that already were tinged with gray. These features though were not the first to be noticed by a stranger. Her large, brown eyes narrowed at the corners like those of a cat, and like the wholeness of Atlas she radiated the ancient Egyptian royalty in Dr. Barrett's books.

The queen's blood had not passed into her daughter. That of Jasper diluted the fine lines and made plain all about her. Her only gem sucked at her breast and drew my eye to the point of rudeness. The baby's hair was red and his skin fair. Sudie caught me staring and said in her soft voice, "If you're wonderin' if dat chile's daddy is Yankee or Rebel, it don't matter, cause deh all been heah and deh all gone. It's jes de same."

I began to learn of slavery and war at that moment.

Minor could not get out of bed for eight days after the trying journey. My efforts to nurse him were in vain as Atlas and Sudie took charge of his care. Atlas went to the Tensas and peeled long strips of bark from willow limbs. He rolled these into coils and boiled them in lake water over the hearth. To this potion he added ingredients from his bundle on the travois and allowed me to dose Minor with six swallows every few hours.

We did not suffer for want of food in the first days at Sudie's, but it soon became obvious that her larder was limited. All the remaining slaves on the plantation were just trying to survive, as Mr. Weingard had not been seen in months. Sudie and the girl were living mostly off the kitchen garden and eggs. Garden work is pleasurable to me and became a way that I could contribute to the welfare of our coterie. I spent most mornings tending the peas, pole beans, squash, and melons. Weeds seemed to invade overnight, and each summer shower hatched a new battalion of stinkbugs to join forces with other pests of the field. I was proud because the garden lived, even thrived under my care, and I was able to plant a second crop of most vegetables.

Atlas, too, went to work to see that we did not starve. He could have taught Nimrod. Lathes rived smoothly away from oak staves under the blade of his long cane knife. He fashioned them around stiff vine hoops and added funnel throats at each end to form fish traps as long as the boy was tall. These were weighted down with bricks and soaked in the lake until they would stay on the bottom without the bricks. Atlas carried them then to the river where the catfish ran.

He also made partridge traps from green sticks stacked in the shape of a four-sided pyramid and set the small cages on the edges of the fallow cotton fields. He dug a tunnel from the outside up into the trap and baited it with chopped corn. Several times he caught the whole covey.

As the days passed, Atlas and I in our roles of providers for the group were able to keep food on the table and hold hard times at bay. Then Atlas made a request that brought me closer yet to understanding the evils of slavery.

Sudie helped him explain. She said that most slaves were forbidden from learning to swim. This rule discouraged those who would run away to seek a better life. This country is laced with rivers and bayous, and a fugitive unable to swim soon encountered one of the natural barriers. Thus encumbered, fleeing slaves were quickly pulled down by packs of trained catch dogs. When Atlas learned that I could swim, he asked me to teach Quint. Sudie said, "Jes in case de war sours. Jes in case."

The first swimming lesson lasted less than a minute. I had no intention of teaching Quint to swim in Rainey Lake because of the abundance of alligators, even though they were not bothersome and kept their distance from people. Sudie said Beck saw one catch a deer once when it came to drink. The alligator hung the deer in a brush top in the lake for a week until it melted enough for him to swallow it in chunks. We had more trouble with turtles stealing fish from our stringers than alligators for any reason. Still, since alligators were scarce in the river and it was shallow in this season, it seemed a much better place to learn to swim.

But I did not see any harm in Quint's becoming accustomed to having water on his face by leaning over the back of the old pirogue in the lake. The boat was tied to the bank near the cabin. The water was not knee deep. I stood in the front of the boat and tried to make a game of it by challenging Quint to see how long he could hold his breath. He was eager, plunging his face in beyond his ears. I was counting away the seconds when the alligator surfaced next to Quint. The head was first, as long as my arm, with big cat eyes that focused on the boy. The back rose next, ridged like a giant ebony washboard, followed by the last foot of his tail. The pirogue was much shorter than the alligator. My paralysis lasted until my mind perceived that the reptile was moving toward Quint at a pace almost beyond detection—slower than a garden snail—like the full moon across the sky. I shrieked warnings in high, sharp sounds that my ears had never before heard. The next movement was lightning fast. Quint ran out of air, rose to face the beast, and in two bounds ran over me and secured the high ground, all without a moment's hesitation. There were no more swimming lessons.

Minor did not heal. After several weeks he still spent most of the day in the bed. Sometimes in the cool mornings he would walk to the garden fence, lean on the rails, and watch me work, but the rising heat always drove him back, that and the flies that sought his wound. His appetite for food and conversation was poisoned, and in spite of the best efforts of Sudie and Atlas his body wasted away. Likewise, our relations showed no signs of recovery.

I pondered our fates for hours on end. More than once I started to go for a doctor only to yield to ebbing faith in prayers that would be answered in God's own time. My foolishness covered up the solution that already was before me. I could sense it in side thoughts on occasion, like one glimpses the passing shadow of a buzzard that disappears into the clouds.

Sister Chloe had told me that Minor had been shot in the hip with the ball passing clean through and exiting on the edge of his groin near the joint of the leg. Here lay the obstacle. I was down on my knees trying to sharpen a worn-out hoe with a worn-out file when revelation came in Lemuel's words.

"We were on the edge of the fight when Grant came roaring through Port Gibson. After the

bad whippin' at Champion's Hill, our regiment was scattered to the winds but got gathered back up and was sent to the crossings on Big Black River to cover the retreat of our poor boys. The last bunch of Rebels was pressed hard by the Yanks and we was doin' our best to give 'em some breathin' room to get across to our side of the river. Minor was in a good position behind some logs near the water, and I was down the bank a ways at the end of our line. I couldn't see him, but he told me that the last of the Alabama boys were swimming toward us when one of 'em started to drown. He went down twice and Minor couldn't stand it no more. He jumped up to help the man and that's when a Yank on the far bank shot him."

"That's when a Yank on the far bank shot him!" I threw the file at a chopping block and ran toward the house hollering for Sudie and Atlas. Like Anatilda, I was determined to examine Minor right then.

"Tain't proper. Tain't proper fer you, mam," Sudie protested. This woman, who was born into an indelicate life and knew nothing else, was worried about my propriety.

Minor surely thought I had lost my mind but was too weak to resist. I rolled him over on his side facing the wall and pulled down his britches.

"This cannot be," I said. The wound on his hip was nearly healed. It did not look like a bullet hole to me. I rolled him again. The groin wound festered raw and ugly.

"He was not shot in the hip," I almost shouted. "The ball would have broken his leg. Look, the holes do not even line up. Maybe he injured his hip on a stob when he fell. The Yankee at his front shot him as he stood. The ball entered his groin and there it dwells."

The gravity of this conclusion poured over the three of us and was followed at once by dread of the merciless task now at hand.

As the weeks had passed I had come to better understand Atlas' communications and rarely needed the boy unless the subject dealt with feelings or thoughts that our charades could not unmask. Now even Quint was confused with the old man's efforts to convey his notions. It became clear that he did not want to attempt an operation at this time because the moon was waning. We could not grasp why this was important. For the next two days he seemed to agonize over the man who had shot Minor and asked me many times if I knew anything of him. Of course I did not. In my judgment, Atlas was trying to get into the man's heart. My mother had spoken in hushed tones of an old woman in our village with this gift.

In the night when the moon did not come, Minor nearly died.

The next day Sudie performed the operation to remove the musket ball according to Atlas' instructions, since he could not see up close. While she made tweezers from thin pieces of split cane, Atlas tied Minor's hands and feet to the bedposts, gently but firmly. He did this in a manner that made me think that he had seen men so trussed before. Minor seemed unconscious during most of the ordeal. His eyes remained closed as I mopped his brow. The wound had grown partly together, and Sudie had to probe deep with the sharp cane. When at last she touched the ball, Minor began to grind his teeth in a terrible way. I could not stand this and ran into the dogtrot, but I could still hear him. The noise was such that I thought his teeth would break. When the ball came out Sudie called me back and told me to fold rags. To stop the blood she and Atlas took turns pressing the rags over the wound. They continued in this manner for several hours. Just before dark Atlas painted Minor's groin with iodine, and Sudie sewed the bullet hole shut with a long hair from Chula's tail.

After a few days we began to feel that our prayers for a successful operation had been answered. Minor rallied and began to gain strength. I like to take credit for an idea that made him heal faster.

South of the cabin on a narrow ridge, sugar cane had once been grown to supply the plantation. Juice from the pressed cane was boiled down in a giant kettle that still rested under the remains of a palmetto-thatched arbor. Twice a week I gave Minor salt baths in this kettle.

Carrying water to the kettle was the hardest part. A bank of salt springs ran into the river a quarter-mile away. Deer and other creatures pawed holes in the shore that caught the orange-tinted water. I tried to fashion a harness for Chula that would carry a pail on each side of his back. The harness slipped and Chula did not like the idea in general. Quint and I ended up carrying the pails covered with oilcloths on a pole resting on our shoulders. Seven feet across the top rim, the kettle took us three days to fill. When on the next day we built a fire on one side to warm the water, I told Quint the ancient Romans would be jealous of this luxury in the Tensas Swamp.

Minor overcame his shyness and came to enjoy the early evening rides to the kettle. By September he could walk the distance and ride Chula back to the cabin. His high spirits were on the mend, and he would tease me about boiling him alive like a cannibal. Then, too, he began to look into my eyes again.

With the improving prospects of our situation I lengthened the tether on my hopes and allowed them to roam beyond the confines of the next day or week. The idea of a future, something that had escaped me for months, filled my thoughts as they had in another time. A biding serenity enveloped me. This lasted until the first of three visits from outsiders to our refuge. Of these, the devil danced at two of the affairs and laughed heartily at the other.

Lucky snake doctors had perched on the ends of our poles and brought fish to our hooks on the day the first visitors walked into the yard. In a similar fashion, the smell of frying fish lured the five former slaves to the pot of boiling lard. They were a loud and rough-looking crew, and their raucousness drew all the members of our household. Two of the five carried rusty shotguns, one had a broken sword, and they wore a hodge-podge of mismatched uniforms from both armies. Sudie and Atlas were particularly anxious of their presence and seemed to sense a danger that was not at first evident to Minor and me.

The gang gathered around the fire and stared at the fixins. Sudie tried to be polite and asked if they were hungry. Their leader, the one with the sword, looked us over as if to size up our group. He glared hard at Minor, who stood in the deep shade of the porch, and reached and grabbed a handful of fish from the wooden tray on the ground.

"Take 'em," Sudie said. She picked up the tray and handed it to the man with the sword. "De res be done now." She ladled the other fish out of the pot and set them to drain on palmetto leaves. The other men pushed and shoved to get at the hot fish.

The leader directed his question to Atlas. "Who dat white man?" Before Atlas could respond, Minor stepped off the porch and walked close to face the men.

"I am Minor Barrett, and I am a privileged guest of these good people. Since you and your friends here have eaten our supper, the least you can do is identify yourselves and your business in these parts."

The headman took a step back and thought for a moment before he spoke. "Well, I reckons I can. Jes call me Dalkeit'. Dis heah Big and Little Hermione." He pointed to the men with the guns.

"Dis Omega and de special man is Frisbee." The men laughed and carried on to hear themselves named after the plantations of their former masters.

Dalkeith continued. "Massa Barrett, how come a fine white man like yoself livin' wid dese high-steppin' niggers? Dey looks like a fresh whippin' up by de massa would do 'em good."

"Not all slave owners are cruel," Minor said. "This very plantation is owned by a fair and kind man."

Dalkeith looked hard into Minor's eyes. "You eber own a slave, Massa Barrett?"

"I have not," Minor answered.

Dalkeith lined his men up with rough shoves and faced them away from us. One by one he raised their shirts to reveal healed scars. His own back was braided with the raised welts of a hundred whippings. "Any man dat will own anuder has got it in him," he hissed. "Some jes keep it deeper down in de craw."

His words forced me to focus on injustices already in plain view. There were scars on Atlas' back, old ones, but scars of the whip still. And Sudie's were light colored and spilled down her arms from beneath the short sleeves of her dress. The idea that I had been seeing around these signs angered me all of a sudden.

Dalkeith changed the subject. "Any mo vittles about? We uns ain't filled yet. Gotta be strong for de las' nigger job." He strutted like a Plymouth rooster when he talked.

"We livin' off de garden. Ain't nothin' cooked," said Sudie.

One of the men headed for the garden and came back hollering about the melons. In great anticipation Quint had picked the first ripe one the day before, and we had looked forward to the sweet afternoon treats. It was not to be. The gang rushed to the patch and began busting every melon looking for the ripe ones. They pulled out the hearts and left the rest to rot.

While they raided the garden we were able to talk and plan among ourselves. Sudie was mad enough to skin them alive. She vowed to tackle them barehanded if they tried to enter her house. Minor said he thought their guns would not shoot because they were rusty, and he did not see caps on the nipples. Atlas sent Quint for the pole-ax, hatchet, and his cane knife, our only weapons. We hid these under the edge of the porch. All agreed that we should talk them away from this place, especially before darkness came.

They came back from the garden carrying armloads of squash. Dalkeith ordered Mirah, who was terrified to near palsy of the strangers, to fetch him some corn meal. Sudie nodded and Mirah ran into the house to retrieve the small sack of yellow meal. I did not like the way Dalkeith looked at Mirah when she returned.

The man called Omega cut up the squash, rolled them in the meal, and threw them in the hot grease to fry. While he cooked, Dalkeith boasted of their plans.

He said he was sorry for taking our food but remorse was not in his heart. He said they were soon to be rich men and would pay us many times over for the vittles. According to his tale they were on their way to Frisbee Plantation several miles downstream to claim a treasure. Months earlier the plantation owner, when warned of approaching Yankees, had loaded a large plantation bell of solid silver into a dray and drove off into the swamp accompanied by two slaves. The master returned without the bell or the slaves. Everyone suspected that the slaves were buried in the hole they dug along with the bell. The Yankees came and razed the place, the owner escaped, and the remaining slaves drifted away. A few people had heard the story and searched for the bell without luck. Dalkeith held that the man called Frisbee had found the burial site a few days later while hunting for a lost cow. Wolves had scratched away the brush used to hide the fresh earth. Frisbee feared haints and quickly ran away. Now they were going to recover the bell and live a carefree life as rich men.

"Gonna sell dat bell, buy fine race hosses, head nawth!" Dalkeith bragged. "Gonna live in a brick house so's my seegar smokin' won't burn it down." The starry-eyed gang erupted into a fit of laughter-drenched amens.

In spite of their amens and claims of going to Frisbee Plantation, I thought they were headed straight to Hell. Most of them could not utter a dozen words without taking the Lord's name in vain. They proved me right.

They ate all the squash and gathered in the late afternoon heat under the shade of a big striped oak to settle their dinner. As they dozed we sat on the porch and watched and waited and hoped they would soon leave. After an hour the gang stirred and talked in low voices that we could not understand. When Mirah's baby cried in hunger from the cabin, Dalkeith jumped to his feet and demanded, "Who's dat baby?"

Sudie pointed to Mirah as she went to tend the child, and Dalkeith exploded in rage. He screamed, "Ain't no time fer a suckler!" He hooked the pommel of his sword under the ear of the iron pot and dumped the hot grease into the dirt. His temper carried him into rantings of profanity. From this madness we were able to detect that he had planned to kidnap Mirah when they left, and a baby was not part of the scheme. The other men stood about uneasy as the tirade continued, no less intimidated than we.

Suddenly the fit passed, the shouting stopped, and the devil in this man took a new and determined course. He walked to the porch steps and declared in a calm tone almost as a father would speak of his own child, "I be minding the young 'un now."

Sudie stood at the top of the steps and Dalkeith struck her down with his fist as he made for the baby. Minor moved to block his way in the dogtrot but Dalkeith pushed him hard against the door. Mirah and the baby screamed inside, but I could not utter even a warning as I watched the broken sword rise above Minor's face and begin its swift and terrible descent.

If Dalkeith had a lucky number, it was not four. That is how many fingers Atlas cut off with the cane knife to save Minor from sure death. So sudden and unexpected was the slash that long seconds passed before Dalkeith realized the nature of his injuries. He fled then from our place, taking his gang and Uncle Jeff, leaving his fingers. We never saw them again.

After a few days Sudie began singing hymns as she worked once more, her pure alto voice melting away our tension and gloom. Not even Chula could hang his head when she sang Wrestlin' Jacob and Roll Jordan Roll. She had a spirit that would not stay down or allow us to wallow in the situation. Her view was, "People don't know better ain't gonna do better." Minor said it was a wonder the screech owls around her cabin did not warble like mockingbirds.

Chapter 13

There were new peculiarities about Minor caused by the war that were hard for me to understand. He was loath to talk about the fighting, and the glimpses of his burdens came seldom and unexpectedly. One evening we were all sitting on the porch after supper watching fireflies and debating whether they or stars were bigger. It was the first day of the year that smelled of autumn, the same as when Mother gave me to the Carters. Atlas and Sudie and Minor were trying to smoke rabbit tobacco in their corncob pipes, but it was too green to stay lit for very long. Mirah sat on the rough planks and leaned back against the locust post, enjoying relief from her sleeping baby. Mirah rarely spoke unless asked a direct question, but out of the blue she said, "Massa Barrett, you ever kill a Yankee?"

Sudie was quick to shush her, nearly spitting the pipe across the porch. I thought for Mirah to ask this bold question she must have had a particularly keen interest in the health of Yankees. I could not figure if her stock was for them or against them.

"Sweet Mirah," Minor began, "I reckon I shot several, but besides one I don't know how many of 'em were killed." He went on to say that in the last year more than five hundred hot balls left the barrel of his favorite but now lost rifle. Many were fired in fear, some in boredom, few in celebration. "Most," he said, "were shot at Chickasaw Bayou north of Vicksburg when Sherman's men paid us a call three days after Christmas. They planned to storm the lines and crack the fortress, but they didn't know that our spies had days before discovered their eighty gunboats and transports steaming our way. We were ready for them, and it was no surprise when the drummers and fifers began to stage their troops in the clear morning air. The abatis along the bayou slowed the Yankees considerably. When they charged up the hill, they were muddier than hogs in a summer wallow after floundering through the natural defense of the lowland sloughs. They came up to us with hot blood and fresh hope. Both were spilt in the yellow dirt in less time than it takes to sing all the verses of Amazing Grace. One wave of mudcoats got nearly to the top when our Sergeant Beard jumped the rampart and ran down to meet them, crowing like a rooster set afire. He shot the color bearer and was himself cut down by a dozen slugs seconds later. For reasons still unfathomable to me, I found myself kneeling over the color-bearer trying to pry the flag from beneath him. It seems now that the next events happened in slow time and in a world without sound. The boy turned over from his belly as if to aid my efforts. He was shot in the neck and strikingly resembled my redheaded second cousin from New Orleans. From the corner of my vision I saw the sweep of a long-barreled pistol as he brought it to bear on the point of my nose. The cylinder was larger than a goose egg, and the single remaining cartridge rolled beneath the firing pin as he thumbed the hammer. I grabbed the barrel and forced it hard toward his mouth. The flash that followed rendered me completely deaf and partially blind for several hours."

Minor gave up on smoking the pipe and said that the battle accomplished nothing in the long run other than sending a bunch of boys to their maker and taker. "That fight, and Vicksburg's still lost," he said. He said the boys in his regiment were proud of the captured flag he brought in. It had flown over a rough bunch of Hoosiers from Indiana. That night the company voted to make Minor the new sergeant, but he declined to take the position. He said he had lost his gumption to lead men to kill the resemblances of his redheaded cousin.

Mirah got up and resituated on the steps where she could get a better view of the night sky. Inside the cabin her baby began to fuss. After a while she said, "I believe stars *are* biggern' lightnin' bugs, Massa Barrett."

Sometime later Sudie sent us to the Tensas to gather a bucket of mussel shells, which she used to scrape everything from calabashes to coon hides. As Minor and I walked along, he suddenly commenced to have a fit, or so it looked to me. He jerked off his hat and began to flog himself about the back of his head. He cussed like the devil's fireman while stomping a cripple jig in the middle of the road. My first thoughts were that a yellow jacket or a red glistener had stung him. It was not so. To him the enemy was a harmless green and black striped caterpillar that he finally mashed into the gumbo clay. When he composed himself, he looked at me, unable to cover his embarrassment, and said, "I'd rather fight a gross of panthers than be measured again." I sat him on a red gum log and got this story.

On the morning of the day that he got shot on the Big Black River, Minor was hoping that the fallback into the Vicksburg lines would go quickly and without trouble. He had a powerful urge to add fresh fish to his meager rations, and for the first time in many days the opportunity was at hand. From his position he could see the swirls of catfish and bream as they feasted on the freshly hatched oak worms falling from the overhanging trees. He felt his breast pocket to be sure he had not lost the small linen bag containing the silk line and bent pins, and for a pole he eyed a tall cane patch just upstream a ways.

Across the field on the far side of the river the Yankee snipers with their long sharpshooter rifles had other ideas. They aggravated the Confederate retreat by picking off the southern soldiers just often enough not to reveal their own positions in the distant treetops. It was one of these skulkers that shot Minor when he left cover to help the drowning Alabama boy.

The ball that struck Minor was not as big as most musket balls, but it was powerful enough to knock him back over the log where he landed on his back and also on the sharpened end of a frog gig that he had been whittlin' to pass the time. Getting shot did not feel like Minor thought it would. He said he expected it to be a pain akin to a bad burn with a hot poker, but this was more like a hard, unforeseen horse kick.

Without even trying Minor knew he could not walk, much less run to dodge the sniper's lead hornets. The other boys in his company were scattered along the riverbank. None were close enough to see his situation, and he did not anticipate a chance of relief until mid-afternoon when Lemuel had promised a visit to reckon on the fishing possibilities if all was quiet at his duty post. Minor plugged the musket ball hole the best he could with a piece of dirty shirtsleeve to slow the bleeding and decided to wait, his only real choice.

In the beginning Minor did not believe he was going to die. He had his haversack that contained, among other things, a boiled potato and a half-full canteen. But by late afternoon his mood soured. His water was long since gone, firing had picked up along the riverbank on both sides, and Lemuel had not come. Then a paralysis fell upon him, seizing his joints, and staking him even more helplessly to the ground. When an inch-worm fell on the back of Minor's hand and began his work, an invisible black mantle settled over the Barrett spirit and began to smother the hope within.

The business of the caterpillar was to measure in his hump-back, jerk-straight way. He started at Minor's remaining cuff and paced up his arm toward his shoulder. Before the worm reached his elbow, Minor saw before him the image of the bow-legged tailor from Farmerville standing over his father's body as it lay straight and gray on a door supported by saw-horses in the sunlit parlor. The tailor stretched his tape along Mr. Barrett's sleeve to measure for the new funeral coat. Just like Minor's caterpillar, he traced the distance around the neck twice to double check, and then surveyed the other sleeve in case one arm was longer, as is not uncommon in backwoods communities where kin marry as often as not. When Minor's worm reached the end of the torn sleeve he reared up as if confused about the great discrepancy and turned about to retrace his steps to settle the matter for all time. To Minor it seemed that he was being measured for his death suit too.

The story was finished. Minor stood up and started walking toward the Tensas again. He went just a few steps before he turned to me and said, "There's another thing I'd just as soon not be measured now, and that's my worth as a man. It's not rightly clear in my mind."

These words pulled me even closer to him as I realized that I did not tote the only sack of old doubts in Louisiana.

Our next visitor was alone and blacker than the wild bunch. We had heard that he was in the area and half expected him to show up. When he came in the night, the end-of-summer locusts hushed, which naturally roused the dogs. They startled the bear and drove him from the leftovers of the garden before he could do serious damage. The next morning Atlas and Minor studied his four-toed hind foot track in the dust and declared the invader to be a half-grown he-bear that would surely return as he had tasted a pumpkin. They decided to catch him.

Sudie was happy. Dalkeith had dumped the last of our lard on the ground. For the weeks since, our meals were boiled and lacked the flavor of her golden brown batters. Sudie said bear oil was sweeter than that of any hog on the Tensas and would not go rancid in the heat. She encouraged the bear catchers.

Quint was excited to the point of getting in the way. He needed a distraction, as he still grieved over the loss of Uncle Jeff and declared several times a day that he hoped the goat with a mighty butt would crack Dalkeith's head. I did not mention my fear that Uncle Jeff had long since been served up as stringy, strong-tasting roasts. To keep Quint occupied, Atlas put him to work making three long spears from bitter-pecan saplings. The hard wood dulled his homemade jack-knife but not his enthusiasm.

Mirah was terrified, according to her nature as I had come to learn. I was unsettled too. I was not frightened of a live bear. A few still roamed the l'Outre bottoms and raided sweet corn patches and bee skeps from time to time. I never knew of a bear to attack a person unprovoked. It was dead bears that stirred a dark stream of thoughts that led back to my mother's village. When I was a small girl a trader had come leading a gray horse that pulled a sled. On the sled was a skinned bear without a head. It looked like a decapitated man. The whole village went into an uproar and drove the trader away. Fires were built and smothered with special green plants. The old people prayed. Mother said that a bear's head should never be cut off until it is completely butchered or bad things would happen. They knew this even before we learned of the pale horse in the Book of Revelation. These thoughts were still in my mind when I made Minor promise not to cut off the bear's head until very last.

Before the war got close, a shallow draft steamboat with the name of *Silver Moon* had run the Tensas River during high water to serve the local plantations. On her last trip she had knocked one of her stacks off on a fresh-leaned ash just below Rainey Lake. Atlas and Minor used the wire cable that had braced the stack to make a snare. They made a loop and ran the cable through two holes in an old door hinge that was rusted half shut. The hinge would allow the loop to close but not open. Minor took down three rails from the garden fence and arranged them in the fashion of a funnel to guide the bear through the gap. Atlas put a small log across the opening for the bear to step over and set the snare close by the log. They tied the loose end of the cable to the ear of the iron wash pot and filled it full of dirt. I watched them, half amused, and doubted their scheme would be successful.

Atlas made gestures to show us that the bear would step in the snare with his front foot and pick it straight up out of the trap. The sweeping motion of the hind leg would be his undoing according to Atlas. Atlas also said it would take several nights to catch the bear. Both of his forecasts were wrong.

The lure of the garden was sweetened with heads and entrails of catfish, drawing the bear in on the first night. The dogs were shut up in the corncrib so as to keep them from harassing the culprit. To my amazement he promptly caught himself just before dawn.

A clatter of tumbling fence rails woke us. Quint was up and racing for his spears almost before Minor caught him by the britches. Everybody else got dressed and went to the porch except Mirah. She burrowed deep under the covers with her baby and did not come out until it was over. We stood close and still and listened to the muted sounds coming from the garden. My heart was not the only one pounding with excitement. Minor did not help the situation when he declared, "Might be grandpappy's grandpappy out there." When the first gray light came, our regiment advanced armed with the weapons of our fortress – spears, axes, and a cane knife proven in battle.

Except for one thing the trap had worked as planned. The only bad idea was the wash pot. It did not slow the bear down much as according to the signs he had quickly dumped out the dirt, crossed the fallow field, and passed through the wall of the forest with the pot in tow. We followed the drag marks to the edge of the big woods, still blanketed in dark shadows that would only brighten by a degree at midday. Here Sudie decided to go back and stay with Mirah. I cannot be sure, but I do not think she was really afraid. Not bold Sudie. She left us with a warning. "Watch yer hind side. Dat bear be mighty roused havin' to tote de pot he gonna be cooked in. Worsen' diggin' yer own grave."

Atlas used the cane knife to open a passage through the briars at the forest edge, and we followed in single file, Quint holding tight to my coattail. Behind the wall the forest floor was cleaner, the drag marks were clear, and we tracked the bear as fast as we could walk. When the trail came to a big rock elm log, it did seem as though the bear reached down and began to tote the pot. Minor said this, and we all looked ahead half expecting to see the bear standing on his hind legs carrying the pot in his arms and staring over his shoulder at us in disdain. I began not to like the situation in a different way, one that favored the bear.

The trail led into a canebrake that ran down a narrow ridge between Rainey Lake and the river. This obstacle slowed us and finally brought us to a halt when the thicket became impenetrable with crossed and leaning canes that wove a barrier no less daunting than castle walls. That the encumbered bear could navigate the maze was supernatural to me. We managed to make our way to the boundary of the canebrake, and Atlas went ahead skirting the edge to hunt the trail if it came out. While we rested, I began to worry that the bear would escape and forever be burdened with the pot meant to cook him. I believe that the river of feelings in some animals flows through the depths of terror no less than in people.

The bear did not escape. Atlas returned and motioned us to follow him quietly. The trail left the canebrake and crossed a slave ditch dug in vain effort to drain Rainey Lake. It went down the river road a ways marking the bare ground with scuffs and drops of blood. It went off the high bank and ended fifty feet from the river. Atlas stopped and pointed ahead. The top of a gum sapling shook from time to time revealing the bear's location. We slipped forward and saw him.

Atlas was wrong in that the bear was not caught by the hind foot. The snare was on his front paw, but just barely, catching the two inside toes. The pot was wedged between two saplings, and he seemed to be pointing at it with his outstretched arm as he strained against the cable. He had known hard times before this day. A long, festering cut lay along his right flank, stressing the general gauntness of his frame. His fur was dull, matted with cockleburs of the fields, and stank to high Heaven. He panted like a dog and turned his head to watch us through small brown eyes. In the minutes to follow I saw in those eyes resolve, panic, and in the end a wild, emerald fire.

The bear did not move or utter a sound as we approached him. Atlas led Quint forward with a hand on his shoulder and made motions to show him how to thrust the spear into the bear's heart just behind and below the outstretched arm. Though the spear was six feet long, Quint whispered that he thought it too short to do the job. It was the beginning of the end of his enthusiasm. Atlas nudged him ahead just as the boy's bones turned to mayhaw jelly. He let the spear drop and brush against the bear's back. In an instant the bear spun around snorting, baring and popping his fangs in the most ferocious manner. We fell all over ourselves in retreat at the fright. Even Atlas's dignity received a minor wound, perhaps justly, for encouraging young Quint.

The bear resumed his former position and was quiet again. It occurred to me that if he charged back through the two saplings the pot would dislodge and he would be able to maneuver again. Minor noticed this too and made me stay behind him. By now Quint was almost out of slingshot range while Atlas squatted on his haunches and studied the bear. I implored Atlas to make quick work of the job at hand, for a suffering creature I cannot tolerate. Minor volunteered to dispatch the bear, but I protested. He was still far from strong and could not run. Already the morning's exertion had made him sallow in appearance. Atlas did not hurry the situation. The air filled with wet heat, and the bear waited in a small cloud of flies. I knew he was in-between life and the unknown. I sensed that he knew more than we could imagine.

Atlas stood up tall with a spear in one hand and the cane knife in the other. He called Quint from the high bank and traded him the cane knife for his plaited palmetto hat. To Quint's great relief he was released to serve as rear guard once again. The next moments are still unbelievable to me. With the spear held high Atlas closed with the bear, talking to him in words that we could not decipher. The bear answered his challenge as before, but Atlas stood his ground and rapped the bear twice on the nose with the spear. When the bear shied away Atlas moved in and began to thoroughly thrash his rear with Quint's hat. A sequence developed and was repeated five times. As the bear turned on Atlas, he received the spear across the nose; when he cowered, Atlas spanked him unmercifully. Finally agitated to a permanent state of panic, he sulked. Atlas reached in with the point of the spear, shoved it under the snare, and pried it loose. The bear knew at once that he was emancipated. Atlas slapped him one final time, tearing the brim from the hat. I could have touched the bear as he raced by me toward the river. For a second he looked up at me and I saw in him a survivor of the ages.

Atlas watched him splash across the shallow river and fade into the undergrowth before he turned to us. Through his beaming smile and shining toothless gums his proclamation rang clear and true. "Freedom!" he declared. I think he had practiced saying this word.

We had no cooking oil for the remainder of our stay at Rainey Lake. After hearing our story Sudie said we all needed "chidn' like a red-headed stepchile." Of course she calmed down soon and before nightfall decided, "Dat bear jes tryin' to make a livin' like de res of us." Mirah was overjoyed that we had returned empty-handed and her wish had come true. Atlas' harmless flogging drove the bear away for good. Minor said the bear was probably too embarrassed to show up here again.

Chapter 14

As predicted by Sudie when the squirrels began cutting green pecans, autumn came early to the Tensas swamp in 1863. Rainey Lake was ringed by giant cypress trees—Choctaw call them shankolo—whose leaves resemble delicate green feathers. Soon after the first cool north breezes they turn burnt orange in the frame of a deep blue sky. Always this scene reminds me of the only story that has come down to me from my father's mother. I heard it third-hand from my mother. Grandmother's tale was of the largest cypress tree in the country where her people had lived. It stood alone on the inside bend of a small clear creek. Two earthen mounds rose from the opposite bank. The titan was a double tree that grew together as lovers in an embrace. Far above the canopy of the surrounding forest their bodies separated for a short span before entwining once more into the crown. Through this hole a single shaft of light flowed at sunrise on the longest day of summer. A basket set atop a pole on one of the mounds captured the magic sunbeam that was quickly spirited away for safekeeping by a wise man of the village. That is all I know of the story, but from the time I first heard it as a small girl I have yearned to find the sacred tree. Minor said that we would search for it some day. He began to say other encouraging things to me also as the autumn weather restored his health.

The sugar kettle therapy continued even though Minor's wound was healed on the outside and he was able to help tote water and wood. Often in these sessions my thoughts would stampede. I would watch Minor undress and become nearly smothered in out-of-control emotions. Like a pair of run-away horses we fast approached a cliff. One evening as he waited for the water to cool a bit, I asked a question that had long been on my mind, "Minor Barrett, what was the whole of your original plan?"

"I had no plan beyond the wedding and my enlistment. Early on I prayed for a revealing epiphany, but as days passed I learned that my fate was bound to the winds of war. And so it was," he said.

"But what now though?" I asked.

He walked to the edge of the firelight, turned, and came back to take my hands. A wild, almost violent passion consumed us. We both took liberties with abandon. On this night I bathed with Minor in the sugar kettle for the first time. In the end he drank me like sweet milk. This was his saying, but I felt it so.

To say that this episode changed our relationship would be an understatement. Questions were answered, doubts vanquished, and the air between us became saturated with an agitated excitement. I am not high-strung, but in this period my nerves were raw. I rose in the morning with one goal—to end the day with Minor in the sugar kettle. I may have acted a fool, but it did not seem so then. The passions of my body overpowered those of my mind and controlled my reasoning. I was ashamed of my hair that had just begun to recover from the Vicksburg shearing. I was proud of the way my breasts roused to my thoughts during the day and gave Minor every opportunity to notice them in this state. When he did, it worked him up.

We began to go to the kettle well before dark because the nights were getting much cooler and it took a while longer to heat the water. On some evenings our passions tended to boil faster than the water. Anticipation enhanced our desires to no end. The kettle was seven feet across and more than three feet deep when it was full. It barely contained our lust. Minor told me of a deck of bawdy playing cards that he had seen in the army. A sergeant said they were from Paris, France. Minor was bashful, but in my way I made him describe them in detail. Then we experimented with all of the scenes on the cards that he could remember. Thus we carried on until the water cooled or exhaustion drove us back to the cabin. None of this seemed wrong then or now.

Atlas and Sudie suspected our new intimacy, and though they did not say much, I knew they did not approve of it under the circumstances. One morning Sudie examined a scratch on my cheek from the rough edge of the sugar kettle and said while walking away, "Look like a yeller barn cat after de full moon." I was glad she could not see my back or Minor's. We called on our trysting place steadily for two weeks until the first of November, when the final sojourner came to Rainey Lake.

The visitor was Butcherman, and he brought death in his oxcart. We had been at Rainey Lake long enough for word of our presence to spread among the freed slaves up and down the Tensas River. With the persistence of a cold-nosed blue tick hound he trailed the rumors to Sudie's cabin. He came during a heavy rain and was already in the yard before anyone noticed. Mirah went to the door when the dogs finally barked and announced the arrival of a white stranger in a wagon with pretty wheels.

He stepped onto the porch and asked of Sudie who stood in the doorway, "Mind if I drip heah on yer porch until this toad strangler passes?"

Sudie nodded and he began to pull off his oilskins as the rest of us filed out into the dogtrot to look him over. I was not surprised at his coming. In the back of my mind I half expected and dreaded it in a way that I cannot explain. He was one of the gatekeepers, always in a position to alter the journeys of those whose paths he crossed, especially if a gain was in sight. His works were not restricted to butchering and tending ferries.

He recognized me and figured out Minor. "Howdy agin Missy," he said to me, "and you must be Mr. Barrett, fully resurrected." I had told Minor of my encounter with Butcherman. He wore morocco-topped boots, a favorite of stylish, rich men, but they did not raise his class even a quarter-notch. His beard was shorter, barely covering a dozen deep smallpox scars. Now that he was here in the flesh and blood, as loathsome as it was, instead of wandering around in the darker places of my imagination, I was not afraid of him.

Minor was short with him. "What brings you to these parts?" he asked.

Butcherman would not look straight at a man when he talked. He directed his answer to the bottom log on the porch. "Well, a freight job brung me close, and when I started hearin' tales of a gal with a blind mule nursin' a soldier over heah on the Tensas, my curosities got riled. If my hunches wuz right I figured a business opportunity gratifying to all parties might crop up. From the looks of things heah my reckonings is pert near on track."

Sudie shook her head and said, "I wish de Lawd'd make ever man speak out de front a his mouth."

"Sir, what business pertaining to us would make it worth your while to seek us out?" Minor asked.

"Mr. Barrett, my wares today is news. I'm peddlin' mighty peculiar tidins' from Iron Branch and gamblin' that you all are in need of a hundredweight."

Butcherman carried in his head that thing most dear to Minor and me at the time, and he knew it from the looks on our faces the moment he revealed his merchandise. We were desperate to learn the state of affairs at home.

The rain turned into Noah's torrents. "You may as well spend the night now. You can bed down here in the dogtrot," Minor told him. "We'll consider your story after supper."

Butcherman unhitched the ox, fed him cottonseed from a sack in the cart, and staked him in front of the cabin. Sudie's beans had been simmering all day when she ladled them out into new sassafras bowls carved by Minor and Quint. Butcherman had three helpings. Not a word was spoken by anyone during the meal.

Minor stoked the fire and offered Butcherman the stool nearest its heat. "Sir, what is your price for news from Iron Branch? News of substance that is, that would be of interest to refugees such as we are," Minor asked.

Butcherman stood up and talked to the hearth. "Nothin' much of value these days ceptin' gold. Scrip don't even make good kindlin'."

"I have got gold!" I blurted out without thinking, and Minor's sudden frown affirmed my foolishness. Butcherman was unsuccessful in hiding his pleasure at the prospects.

Minor took charge again. "You will be compensated fairly for your detour. That I can promise. Beyond this, the situation is in your hands."

Butcherman allowed that he would take a chance with our fairness and began a story that would cause us to hurry from the great forests of the

Tensas, the nosi aiasha of my mother, the place where acorns abound.

Butcherman said he had traveled to Claiborne Parish to discuss the freight contract in which he was now engaged. While there, Yankee soldiers from the east occupied Monroe for several days, blocking his normal route of return. To avoid them he returned on the north road from Homer through Farmerville and stayed the night at the livery stable in Iron Branch. Old Mr. Colvin gave him the news.

Anatilda had returned to Iron Branch in a state of terrible despair. She told of rescuing Minor from a prison hospital only to see him drown before her very eyes as they tried to cross the Mississippi River at night. It was a damned Yankee gunboat that rammed her skiff, she claimed, and she and Mink barely escaped alive.

In a rough-cut way, Butcherman was capable of compassion. It seeped from his voice as he told of Minor's mother. When Mrs. Barrett heard Anatilda's news she took to her bed and died two weeks later. Always fragile in spite of her noble spirit and subject to the fevers, she died of the shock and was buried next to her husband on the sandy ridge that juts out into the l'Outre Swamp.

The news stunned Minor and me. Sudie spoke condolences in her simple way, and Atlas put his huge hand on Minor's shoulder.

"That's the worst of my report," said Butcherman, "but I fear the balance ain't cheerful neither." He went on to tell that Anatilda was making a claim for the Barrett estate, her being the widowed daughter-in-law and closest living kin. Seems the Tubbs were falling on hard times, just like everyone whose wealth was tied to cotton in a big way. Butcherman said he heard that Anatilda would get a hearing at the November court in Farmerville if it was held. Nothing was certain anymore since the Yankee raids on Monroe and Bastrop. He said that was all of his news connected to us.

"Was there talk of my fate?" I asked him. I dreaded the worry I had caused the Carters.

"I didn't hear none directly, Missy, 'ceptin Old Man Colvin said you wuz mostly written off as dead too."

"Court is on the first Tuesday of the month," said Minor. "What day is this?" As time passed on the Tensas, we had lost track of the date.

Butcherman said he was sure this night was Saturday, the third of November 1863.

Puffs of smoke swirled back down the chimney and into the room. Just as the weather changed, so too did our lives. Minor said we would leave the next morning at first light. He did not want to talk any more then, and we all went to bed. Butcherman slept alone in the dogtrot. Sudie double-checked the latchstrings to be sure they were pulled in.

Everyone stirred early. Sudie cooked, Minor and I collected our few belongings, Quint brought up Chula, and Atlas curried him with a mussel shell comb. Butcherman said he was headed back to Claiborne Parish through Monroe, figuring the Yankees were done with their raiding there for a while being's it was so far from their main force. He claimed to know the favorable stream crossings on this route and allowed that our company would be welcome. Minor accepted his invitation as long as progress was satisfactory. Atlas and Quint decided to escort us for a half day.

The sun rose on a clearing sky, the last clouds chased away by a brisk wind of the far north. Trees still dripped from the evening storm as if to mock the tears of our sad farewells. I hugged Sudie and Mirah for a long time. Sudie urged me to remain ever cautious. To press her point she chilled me to the bone by telling me that Dalkeith had planned to take me too. Mirah cried when I gave her my red hair ribbons and ran to adorn her baby. The handfuls of gold coins that I left in the churn could not begin to repay our dark champions. Before I knew them, I had worried that the Bible did not mention Indians, but after discovering that angels could be black I felt better for myself.

The ox bawled in the yoke when Butcherman cracked his whip and started the cart's rainbow wheels rolling north along the riverbank. We followed behind the cart in the mud, each of us with thoughts of the past and future. Only young Quint dwelled in the present as he roamed the trail gathering the wind's bounty of freshly fallen sweet pecans.

Before noon we reached the rain-swollen ford on the Tensas. Butcherman said we would not be able to cross in another hour. He was right. The water was above my waist, and I had to hold fast to the back of the cart to keep my feet. From the far bank our dear friends waved their last goodbyes, Atlas' toothless grin forever a treasured memory. The road kept north, still against the river.

In my innocence or ignorance I had not until then realized that Minor's plan was to be in Farmerville for the Tuesday court if it was held. The notion came to me with his growing impatience at the pace of our journey. According to Butcherman, the ox had one gait and no amount of abuse or reward would hasten his step. Butcherman figured we could make it in time if we traveled part of the night. He said jayhawkers and other bandits roamed the country and it would be safer if we stayed together. He said he had a good pistol under the seat for our protection. Then he said something that led me to swear that I would be nowhere near him or his cart when darkness came.

Minor asked him, "Would thieves consider your cargo valuable? Perhaps we are subject to added danger by being in your company." I had paid no attention to the lumps beneath the cotton sacks in the cart.

"My freight today wouldn't interest any but a starvin' hog. And as a man right familiar with swine likes and dislikes, that's saying a heap." Butcherman reached back and pulled the cotton sacks aside to reveal two pine coffins. Rapping his knuckles on the closest, he continued, "My apologizes fer neglectin' the formal introductions, but I figured you didn't have a mind to shake Tommy Ratliff's hand." Butcherman saw that this talk was making Minor mad, so he began to explain. "His old pap sent me to fetch him and bring him home to Claiborne Parish. The boy took sick and died in Mississippi a couple of months ago. Some men from his unit got him as far as Vidalia, and that's where I met him, cached under the Methodist church. He's in right good shape, tarred and packed in charcoal dust, much more agreeable than a hickory-smoked feller I hauled a couple years back. He was a mean 'un. Said his last request was to be buried in a chinquapin coffin so's he could go through Hell a poppin'. I reckon he was paid back in his own coin. The nails is loose if you all want to look Tommy over."

I realized then why Chula had shied away from the cart all day. Unlike me on this occasion he did not need sight to sense an unsettled spirit.

Minor asked about the second coffin. As the ox plodded onward, Butcherman reached behind the seat again and flipped the lid off the other box. "It's waitin' fer a paying customer," he said. "No tellin' what opportunity lies around the next bend of the turnpike."

I grabbed Minor's arm and pulled Chula up short, letting the cart go ahead. "Did you see what was in the open coffin?" I whispered to Minor. "Butchering tools: a meat cleaver, hand axe, bone saw, and knives thin and pointed, thick and blunt— and leg irons. Tell me why a butcher needs two pairs of leg irons. I will not be his next opportunity!"

Minor had never seen me in such a state of panic and tried to calm me. "He's too slow for us anyways," he said. "We'll part company right now if it will ease your mind." I assured him that it would ease my mind considerably.

We paid Butcherman ten dollars in gold, leaving us with six dollars for whatever lay before us. He was satisfied and thanked us for the business. "Might cross your path agin before you know it, if I set my sails for night travelin'," he said. We soon left him behind, Chula high-stepping in the mud and grumbling in the deep holes.

At the Vicksburg-to-Monroe railroad we struck the main road that ran along the track on the south side. There, to our surprise, the ferry on Bayou Macon was operating, served by two young women dressed as men. When Minor asked about the trains, they said none had run since the Yankees raided Monroe. We crossed without troubles and passed through the village of Delhi without stopping. Burned down as it was on the last Christmas Day, it seemed a pitiful place.

The higher ground of the Macon Hills was a welcome sight to swamp-weary travelers. The yellow earth, when wet, did not ball up and stick to shoes until they were pumpkin size like the coal-black soil of the Tensas. We made good time throughout the afternoon, even eating Sudie's baked sweet potatoes while walking steadily onward. The late fall day was short, but as darkness came we approached the high bank of the Boeuf River.

A natural campground under giant elms was situated above the ford. Minor wanted to camp there but decided to stay only after carefully studying the river. Leaves and other sweepings of the stream rode the middle currents, a sign that the rise was over, so we stopped to camp for the night, figuring the ford would still be passable in the morning.

All day long wild fowl had passed over our heads riding the north winds, some calling, others silent. As we gathered firewood and spread our blankets, they began to fall from the sky in whirls of spinning cyclones over an old bed of the river that lay before us. In their language those already on the water beckoned newcomers with enchanted pleadings. Countless wings from every direction answered the appeals until all was muffled in a dull roar. Suddenly shots thundered in their midst. Only a temporary pause in the din disturbed the clamor. The shotguns fired again, flames from three barrels flashing bright in the twilight. Another volley and the hunters were done. The spectacle of thousands continued as before. Minor said Yankee soldiers were like ducks in that there was no end to them.

The night was cold. I spent most of it huddled before the glowing coals trying to think of anything but the last time I camped on the east bank of Boeuf River. The hole in Chula's ear was daily reminder enough. When those thoughts did slip through my prayers and quiet hymns, they seemed to come from a time when I was another person. I wondered if it was possible for as many new things to happen to me in the next four months as had happened in the last four. I wondered if I could confuse the squeak of an oxcart wheel with the calls of baldpate and teal ducks. The scenes playing out in my imagination lasted until almost dawn, fading away before the finale.

Boeuf River was as deep as the Tensas. We crossed early and found the three duck hunters at their roadside camp. Two old men and a boy had just returned from retrieving the birds killed the night before and were drying their clothes before a fire. Dressed in their underdrawers, they paid me no mind and told Minor that nine shots had yielded two grass sacks full of ducks, all they could tote back to the Monroe market after drawing the entrails. Their only noteworthy news was that the road to town was passable but difficult in the Lafourche bottoms.

Out of the swamp again, the road turned northwest to run along Bayou Desiard above Monroe. We followed it through once-rich plantations until the stream emptied into the Ouachita River. Passersby assured us that no steamboats were running the river to any destination, including Farmerville. This news doused our hopes of an easy end to the journey and pressed us harder for time. We crossed the river to Trenton on a cattle barge and began to search for horses to hire. The livery yielded a bay gelding with lampers and a lead on another horse belonging to a woman who lived on the edge of town. She was happy to rent her tall, iron-gray mare for a deposit in gold. Once mounted we took the Arkansas Road through the pine hills, stopping briefly to satisfy Chula who refused to be led by Minor on the gelding. He had no dispute with the mare though and followed her at ease with only small debates concerning the pace.

As we rode along I pointed out to Minor a small clump of Indian pipes growing in the shade of a mulberry. They were no taller than a snuff bottle, without color, and their heads bowed over toward the earth in a manner of gloom. "About the coming events, I am feeling the way they look," I told Minor. "Besides, I must look and smell the part of a wet polecat, between the layers of dust and wood smoke." Minor said I looked just fine to him, but that he would work on the problem.

By evening Minor was confident we could make Farmerville by mid-morning the following day and began to seek shelter for the night. The first house offered beds and a supper of peas and cornbread. The family name was Downs. When we left the next morning, Minor said he felt bad about passing ourselves off to them as cousins.

In the back yard stood a rusty well pump, which served the house and stock on this dry farm. A half-log blackgum pipe beneath the spout caught the tailings and carried them through a worm fence to a big cypress trough worked smooth by some master of the adze. The pump was long primed – it took nearly twenty strokes of the handle to bring up the first cupful. Afterwards, I called it the guinea pump because when worked it cried like a spooked guinea hen. Minor said the slow, short strokes sounded more like a jaybird to him and that it was a shame the people did not properly oil the barrel on such an important implement.

After supper Minor gathered a kettle of water and hung it on a pot hook in the hearth to heat. He signaled me to follow him and led me to the pump where he had arranged a three-legged milking stool, a towel of sorts, a soap cake, and a vial of rose water that he had bought from the woman of the house. "Abita Carter of Bayou de l'Outre," he said, "on this fine, clear night with Orion as our watchman, I will cleanse your spirit."

He sat me on the stool and began to wash my hair. The water was cool enough to draw chill bumps at first but not uncomfortable. It flowed over my shoulders, down my blouse and skirt. No effort was made to keep from wetting me thoroughly. Minor alternated his rhythmic stroking of the pump with those of his fingers through my hair. He tilted my head back to add the soap. It smelled faintly of honey and rose to a fine lather in the soft water. Still the pump handle slowly rose and descended over me, Minor's hands worked, Orion watched, and the jaybird cried. For some moments I left my body to stand to the side and watch this scene. It stirs me yet.

Minor left to retrieve the kettle and returned to rinse me with warm water. I sent him off again to fetch the remains of my simple, clean dress from Chula's pack. Minor brought it; I draped it over the fence and demanded that he sit on the stool for retribution. His hair was nearly to his shoulders, as long as mine, and in dark waves just the same. The flowing water revealed hard muscles returning to his neck, chest and stomach. At some point the silence of the jaybird roused me from this second trance and revealed my hands far from Minor's hair. Minor sneezed suddenly and claimed that he was not owed a drowning. It was his way of moving us along to a more proper level in this setting. Before we went into the house, he daubed the notch in my neck with rose water and just lower too. When he kissed me the worries of the morrow parted as surely as the Red Sea did for Moses.

Chapter 15

Our last obstacle was the D'Arbonne bottoms, a mile-wide swamp that catches the bayou's overflows between the red clay hills. It did not hinder us much. The bayou was not yet out of its banks for the winter, and a new pole road lay in the low spots. We arrived at the landing below town and crossed on the ferry. The one-armed operator told us that court was indeed in session as he was tired already from his morning's business.

The courthouse was a new white-frame building in the center of Farmerville. It faced west so people coming up the hill from the landing on the bayou saw it first before the half-dozen saloons that surrounded it port and starboard. Minor said a favorite topic of discussion in these places was the buzzards that liked to perch on the steep roof of the courthouse and what that meant about the goings-on inside. As on most court days, the square was crowded with both town folks and farmers from the countryside. Soldiering-age boys were scarce though, and the girls and ladies had to settle for the company of old men and a few cripples. We tied the horses and Chula on a side street before marching on. Minor's firm grasp of my hand did little to slow my racing heart.

Court was held in the big front room, and the parish records were kept in a small back chamber. The front door opened into a foyer with steep stairs to the balcony tucked into one corner. Minor and I went directly to the front door and hurried up the stairs. He had his hat pulled down low; I pretended to be his shadow, and no one seemed to notice us. We shared the balcony with three black couples and a half-dozen giggling white boys fresh from a barber. Minor hushed them so we could hear and pulled our bench close to the front rail.

Judge Hezekia Thacker, still adorned with an explosion of gray whiskers, sat behind a table staring at two men arguing before him. The issue was property lines and a blazed persimmon tree. They droned on as I searched the audience of fifty or more. Anatilda stood out. She was dressed in mourning black and sat beside an older woman whom I took to be her mother. Minor spotted Mr. Carter, Lemuel Greenlea, and a few others from Iron Branch. When the judge decided he had heard enough, he told the two men to cut the damned persimmon tree down, split it into stove wood for the school house, and get the property line resurveyed. The men skulked out.

Anatilda's business was next on the docket. The clerk stood up and addressed the judge: "Your honor, the next matter before the Twelfth Judicial Court is the affairs of Mrs. Anatilda Tubbs Barrett and the succession of the Barrett estate." I could tell that it took all of Minor's willpower to keep from leaping over the rail and charging to the front.

The judge ordered the proceedings to begin. The clerk nodded to Anatilda, she went forward, and in spite of swearing before God to tell the truth, lies and deceit filled her practiced drama. She began by telling of her wedding and the cruel war that lured away her gallant, beloved husband. She told of the news of his injury and her desperate efforts to rescue him. Her tale of their joyful reunion in the hospital made my stomach turn. I feared I would be sick there in the balcony. She hurried through the scene of Minor's drowning. Then she reached into her knit handbag and pulled out the death announcement of Mrs. Barrett on a scrap of the *Farmerville Democrat*. Her claim to the Barrett estate, she said, was based on the fact that no wills had been discovered and she was the closest surviving heir according to the French laws of Louisiana. Minor whispered to me through clenched teeth that she was better than some of his old professors.

Judge Thacker listened to Anatilda intently. When she stopped, he did not speak for long moments and seemed deep in thought. Then he called the sheriff over to his big table and they spoke in low tones. Anatilda jumped when the judge finally addressed her, "Mrs. Barrett, as you know we have no official record of your husband's death— only your testimony. This poses a dilemma for the court. Painful though it may be, can you give more specifics of his passing?"

Anatilda was flustered for an instant. "Well he's dead! I saw it with my own eyes," she cried. She had not expected this development. "I myself was nearly killed." She was quick to come to her senses, as I had seen before, and she built a story on the spot. She told of their efforts to cross the treacherous river in between the passing of Yankee boats and how they had almost made it when a slow whirlpool captured them. Everyone in the courtroom hung on her words. A sidewheel packet bore down on their tiny vessel, she continued, and sparks from the pine torch that she desperately waved singed her hair and arms. She drew back the sleeve of her dress to offer the judge imaginary evidence of her wounds. Her arm was long and white, not nearly so dark as mine.

"The Yankees had no watch," she said. "Poor Minor. He lay in the front of our skiff just where the packet struck. The slave and I were thrown into the air away from the tempest." She paused for effect. "Knowing that he suffered little is my only solace."

The judge pondered her words before asking the room, "Is there anyone here today who can affirm or refute this testimony?"

People shuffled and looked around. I knew Minor was waiting for this moment. We were still unnoticed by those below. Slowly he began to stand, but before he was discovered a sudden commotion beneath drew the attention of all. The door burst open and Mink walked down the center aisle to stand in front of the judge.

"I been listening at dat winder, yor honor," he pointed to the closest of two small portals on the north side of the building, "and der's no way under Heaven I can let dis pass widout having my say."

His voice was deep and rich in the hushed courtroom, and I knew I was seeing an act of utmost bravery. Whatever the outcome of the day, Mink could expect nothing but suffering and a good chance of death for his actions.

"My name is Mink. I's Miz Tilda's servant."

Anatilda stood close enough to touch him. I thought her glare would melt him to butter.

"Hellfire the slave testifying rules! Consider yourself under oath," the judge ordered Mink. "Were you a witness to Minor Barrett's death?"

"I reckon I wuz one of de las' persons to see him alive, and he weren't much alive at dat," said Mink. He went on to tell the truth—all of it. He said the boat accident did not happen. He told how Anatilda cast Minor, unconscious and wounded, to the perils of the river. He said the only sidewheel packet he knew about was the one they rode from the Vicksburg landing across to Young's Point the next day.

The judge was as stunned as everyone else in the courtroom. He shuffled the papers on his big desk to break the long silence after Mink's story. His question to Mink seemed born of pure curiosity rather than legal order. "Why would she do that after such exertions to find him?"

Mink was embarrassed when he spoke. "Miz Tilda say he ruint. Say she need a whole husband to tend her proper."

Anatilda was in a state like I had never seen. She looked at the judge and said, "You don't believe that slave, do you? Since when can a nigger testify against a white woman? He's jealous. He made advances. In fact he attacked me in my tent one night on our journey home!"

The court stirred. Doubts and verdicts flew around the room in tight circles like bats in a cistern. I flew with them as Minor dragged me down the stairs pushing people aside in the foyer in a deliberate charge to the front. We stopped beside Mink and directly before Anatilda.

When she could speak, her voice was thick and sweet. "My darling husband. You are alive. Come to me." She reached for him with long white arms. For a lingering moment I thought he was lost to me again.

Judge Thacker slapped his own knee twice in the manner of his behavior at the Scholar's Competition years before.

Minor turned and embraced me. He kissed me on the cheek and then on my mouth until the judge beat his desk with a Colt pistol and demanded order. Yet we remained in this clasp a long time while all about us a chaos of cheers and one solitary wail filled the courtroom.

Chapter 16

Judge Thacker did not stay mad at us. Three months later at the next court session he granted Minor a divorce from Anatilda. He said he figured attempted murder of the first degree was grounds enough.

"What say you, Abita Carter?" These were the words Minor used to ask me to marry him. We were at our special place on Bayou de l'Outre in late spring. The wild canaries had just returned to haunt the streamers of gray moss. We stood on the giant cypress log. "I say yes to you, Minor Barrett," I answered, and my thoughts drifted to the half of the cypress log hidden beneath the water. I imagined a hole in the trunk that beckoned magic sunbeams into a basket for the prosperity of my grandmother's people, of which I was one.

We were married at the Carters' house by a new preacher who had settled in the village. He was mostly John Wesleyan Methodist. I was not the most beautiful woman at the wedding. My mother was. Mrs. Carter sent her a secret invitation, and their hired man brought her from Monroe in the buggy. She was very short. Except for the silver strands mixed in her long black hair, her face looked the same to me. She stood at my side and held tight to my arm as we said the vows.

Being married to Minor was wonderful, but the hard times multiplied for everyone as the war dragged on. When Minor signed the parole papers at Vicksburg, he promised not to fight again until there was an official swapping of prisoners. Early in 1865 a Confederate captain came to Farmerville and posted on the courthouse door a list of Union Parish soldiers whose paroles were lifted and who were ordered under threat of desertion charges to report for duty at Cotile Bayou near Alexandria. Minor's name was on the roll. I begged him not to go. I lied and told him he was not able-bodied. I reminded him that he did not have a horse since the Tubbs had kept the Claybank mare and departed with her in the dark of the night on their exodus to Texas. He filled my arms with wild irises of burnished copper, bought a green-broke, strawberry roan gelding and left in April.

I went to live with the Carters again, and for two months I walked to the cypress log on Bayou de l'Outre at least once a week to pray until Judge Thacker came with a warning of Butcherman. The judge told us a story of a man named Cook who had been in his courtroom the day before. The man had been captured by a fourteen-year-old boy near Marion while trying to steal a plow horse. In the small back chamber of the courthouse Cook pleaded for mercy and offered the judge a tale of a greater felony.

Cook said that a year or so back he fell in with the man we called Butcherman driving his oxcart on the Homer Road a few miles west of Shiloh. That evening, they met up with a soldier and all got drunk on Cook's plum brandy. When the soldier passed out, Butcherman hatched a plan to double his freight money and make good use of an empty coffin. Cook said that Butcherman committed the "high crime" on the soldier and offered to split the extra funds if Cook would go along with the scheme. Cook said he feared for his own life and had no choice. They carried the bodies of Tommy Ratliff and the new soldier to Homer in Claiborne Parish. Tommy's father paid them proper, but when they offered up the new soldier to his family on Sugar Creek, telling them that he was picked up in Vidalia also, troubles began. The man's sister said she had just received a letter from him in which he claimed to be on his way home from Arkansas. The Homer sheriff got suspicious, and Butcherman and Cook decided to donate their services to the family and left town in the night. Before parting ways, Butcherman threatened Cook by telling him that only three people in this world could testify against his story, and he planned to take care of two of them, a lawyer and his half-breed woman over near Iron Branch, soon enough.

After this story, Judge Thacker told Mr. Carter that I should stay close by on the farm and be ever alert. Butcherman's words from the Tensas began haunting me day and night. He had said, "Nothing is more certain than death, and nothing is so uncertain as its time."

On the first day of June 1865, I got up early as usual and hummed my way out the back door in my nightdress and down the path to the cedar-board outhouse. Mr. Carter was already gone to check the crops, and his wife was starting the breakfast fire in the stove with slivers of fat pine. As I reached the outhouse I noticed a movement in the road at the corner of the garden, just where Lemuel had called to me two years earlier. The movement—the flicking ear of an ox—stopped me in my tracks. I took a step back to see around the pole beans and saw the bright wheel of the cart. Before I could act in response, the door of the outhouse burst open and I was in the clutches of Butcherman. Still smelling worse than the foulest hog, he shoved me into the outhouse and barred the door from the outside with the heavy latch that kept out the night-foraging possums. I wailed an animal cry of fear.

"Shut up, you wormy sow. Where's yer educated ruttin' partner? I've got more news for the both of ya, and I'm afeared it's all sad again." Butcherman obviously did not know that Minor had left for the war again.

Suddenly, Mrs. Carter called from the back porch, "Abita, what's the commotion? Is that chicken snake in there again?" Before the end of these words settled on the light dew she screamed, and I heard a crash of pots and dishes in the house.

Mrs. Carter's hand bell, the one she used to call me to morning lessons for many years, rang once and all was quiet. I beat on the door of my prison and alternately pressed my eye to the breast-high knothole in the door. I saw Butcherman when he came out of the house and walked out of my view toward the cart. Moments later, his eye was an inch from mine at the knothole. Where an eye is usually white, his was the yellow of spoiled eggs. Where there is normally color, the gray of wet ashes encircled the window to his condemned soul. I jerked back and slammed my hand over the knothole. The blade of his knife sliced through my palm and out the back of my hand so fast that I felt no pain until he withdrew it.

"Mite dull, don't ya think, Missy? Good iron though. Six inch blade made from a Birmingham hoe with a black hickory handle." His voice was calm, matter-of-fact. "Before I join you in that crapper for our discussion I'm gonna sharpen it a bit. You might want to listen."

I knew very well the sound of a knife blade drawn slowly across a dry whetstone. For long minutes he kept at it while blood from both sides of my hand soaked through the whole front of my nightdress.

"There now," he said. "There ain't enough handle on this sticker to carve a notch for ever critter it's skinned, and that don't even count human varmints." He slid the bar back from the door letting it swing open and slap the outhouse with a dull thud. If I had had my senses about me I could have charged out then and perhaps escaped his intended crime, but I crouched in the back corner holding my wounded hand to my breast.

Butcherman stepped close and stood just across the threshold with the bright, early sun to one side of his head. To me, his silhouette looked black as death. "You got a choice here, Missy." He was looking down and speaking almost softly. "If'n you tell me the whereabouts of that Barrett boy, I'll bar this door again and go on about my business. If'n you squawk loud enough, the old man of this place will turn up and set you loose by and by."

I wished I knew where Minor was at that moment. I wished he would gallop into the yard, jump the garden fence on the strawberry roan and rescue me. It could have happened.

Butcherman continued, "But if you decide to play dumb injun, for starters you and that giant darky on the Tensas is gonna speak the same language. I can't tolerate no loose tongues in these times. And there won't be no readin' or writin' up testimonies for no judge either. That'll take some close work, but you'll likely live if you ain't too thin-blooded." He flipped the knife in his hand. "What's yer answer?"

I did not have a voice much less an answer. It was another of those times in my life when I seemed to be watching my fate from a distance. I saw an in-between girl trapped in an outhouse, about to be mutilated by a madman while hummingbirds twittered and fussed over red honeysuckle on the fence. Her thoughts were not those of the situation at hand but of a man with eyes as dark as hers who would never be in her arms again.

Butcherman came for me then. This time the pain was instant and terrible. With the first blow my arm fell useless to my side, and my neck felt as though it was scalded with boiling water. He butted me and we were awash in blood—and then he lay very still with his head in my lap in the outhouse.

Mrs. Carter had shot us both with her husband's two-barreled derringer. The first ball struck the top of my collarbone breaking it clean. The second cut a deep trough down the side of Butcherman's head, not killing him, but addling him thoroughly until Mr. Carter arrived.

When Minor returned safely to me three days later on the fourth of June, things were mostly sorted out. Butcherman was locked in the Farmerville jail with Cook. My injuries were on the long healing path. Except for a small cut on her forehead and a burden of grief for shooting me, which she carries yet in spite of my pleas, Mrs. Carter was not seriously harmed. By her own account Butcherman never touched her. In her efforts to halt his advances she had turned over the pie safe and knocked down the cupboard before falling against the stove. Poor Minor seemed to suffer more than anyone though, of guilt for not being here to prevent this tragedy. He vowed to attend the trial and see that justice was upheld.

Head bandaged in flour sack rags and shackled in his own leg irons, Butcherman was tried on the first morning of the July docket. Because of the South's surrender politics, it was the last court session in Union Parish for a long time. Cook testified against Butcherman as promised, and Judge Thacker sentenced him to hang the following Thursday, as soon as the old scaffold could be repaired. Cook's trial was in the afternoon. He was found guilty of horse theft. Judge Thacker spoke angrily to him about his part in the soldier's murder, but he kept his word too. He sentenced Cook to ten years in prison, less one day for speaking against Butcherman. Cook never served his sentence, though, at least not Judge Thacker's. Butcherman strangled him to death that night with his head bandage in their jail cell.

Minor and Mr. Carter almost missed the execution. When Judge Thacker heard of the latest crime, he said, "To Hell with the old scaffold. I know of a dammed fine hangin' tree." And he moved the date up to Monday. The tree was an old broke-topped sycamore on the Bayou D'Arbonne side of the courthouse square just up from the ferry. Until the hanging, squealer ducks had nested in its holler every spring, and the low winter light played on the ivory bark in a way that reminded me of nakedness. A single stout limb reaching out from the downhill side is still called the Butcherman's Branch by boys of the town.

The law was abided as the church bell struck ten of the morning. Some while later the oxcart with red and black wheels carried the body of Butcherman to a pauper's grave close beside the man named Cook.

Minor came back home late that afternoon and solemnly announced that the Butcherman of Boyd's Ferry would from that day forward torment only his brothers in Purgatory. I asked Minor and Mr. Carter if the Butcherman had a real name, one that was attached to his soul by his mother at his birth. No one knew of it, they said. I wonder what kind of tragedy could befall a person to cause him to lose his name to the world. Whatever the accident, I hope it was the reason for his evil nature. It makes me feel safer from the devil.

In the time that has passed since the war ended, a gloom has settled on the land. The few large farmers like the Tubbs have mostly left Union Parish. Without their slaves they are land poor. The Carters and other average folks are getting by, being accustomed to feeding themselves. The freed Negroes are suffering the most. Without direction for the first time, many have yet to realize they are responsible for their own lives. They ramble about in search of one Holy Grail after another. Some have taken to stealing almost as often as the sorry white men of the parish. Black and white women and children have come near to starving for want of worthy husbands and fathers. Northern scalawags have drifted in to take advantage of everyone, their politics rubbing salt in open wounds. Uncertainties of the future rise up like revetments on all sides with the people in the middle. Healing remains around some distant bend of a southern road.

Minor tries to support us by practicing the law, but few have money to pay for his services. It is ironic that his principal business is settling the matters of dead soldiers. I am affected by the lack of income less than others because being in-between has always been my life and, as I have recently concluded, my fate. I am not averse to the state, as once was the case, for it has proven to enhance the experience of blessings simple and great. This year we have become partners with the Carters to put in a cotton crop. We live in the house of Minor's mother, where books and the window with one hundred twenty panes surround me. Lemuel, Mink, and other friends visit when they find time. My wounds have healed with the only lingering effect being that I now must churn butter left-handed. Minor suffers a slight limp when he is tired but is otherwise well. As I chop cotton at the Carters', I can watch Chula growing fat and old across the rail fence. And in the cool evenings there is the balm of my anniversary gift, which Minor purchased at the auction of the Tubbs' estate. People say it is the largest sugar kettle in Union Parish. But Minor says its use is necessary to soothe my swelling belly and ease my apprehensions in this, yet latest expression of an in-between life with a particular man.

THE END

Kelby Ouchley is a naturalist and managed National Wildlife Refuges for the U.S. Fish and Wildlife Service for 30 years. His first book, *Flora and Fauna of the Civil War: An Environmental Reference   Guide* (http://www.lsu.edu/lsupress/bookPages/978080713 6881.html), was published by LSU Press in 2010. A collection of his essays, *Bayou-Diversity: Nature and People   in   the   Louisiana   Bayou   Country** (http://lsupress.org/books/detail/bayou-diversity/), was released by LSU Press in 2011. Since 1995, Kelby has written and narrated a weekly natural history program for KEDM 90.3 FM, the public radio station that serves the Ark-La-Miss area. Kelby and his wife, Amy, live in the woods in Rocky Branch, Louisiana, in a cypress house surrounded by white oaks and black hickories. His website is http://bayou-diversity.com/ Signed copies of his books are available through the contact page of this website.

----

*Bayou-Diversity review: "Kelby Ouchley has given us an unforgettable collection of essays on the natural history of Louisiana. Nothing escapes his attention…At the heart is an acute understanding of Louisiana ecology—how it works and should work. The essays are beautifully written…I haven't enjoyed or learned so much about the natural history of a place since I read Aldo Leopold's *A Sand County Almanac.*"

-Phillip Hoose, National Book Award Winning author of *The Race to Save the Lord God Bird*